Worp

Lynn K. Russell

2021 White Bird Publications, LLC

Published in the United States
by White Bird Publications, LLC, Austin, Texas
www.whitebirdpublications.com

Paperback ISBN 978-1-63363-533-3
eBook ISBN 978-1-63363-534-0
Library of Congress Control Number: 2021941556

PRINTED IN THE UNITED STATES OF AMERICA

Dedication

So many wonderful people have taken a part in getting *Worpple* out to children. To the crew at COMPASS thank you for your encouragement and support. To Jill Ebsworth and Judy Tompkins for their suggestions and help. And, to the staff at White Bird Publications for all the work you put in to make this book perfect. Thank you each and every one of you.

Index

Chapter 1

Cam

The hopes and dreams of youth are as delicate as the wings of a butterfly in the wind. Hopes of a better future raced through Cam's mind as he swept the football from the ground in a smooth motion and spun around to face his imaginary opponent. He was practicing football in the hopes of getting on the school team next season. With care, he secured the ball against his body as though it was as precious as his cell phone, and he dashed toward the end of the field. Cam placed the ball on a clump of Earth he was using as a kicking tee. It needed to be placed just right in preparation for a perfect field goal. In his mind, an imaginary goalpost lined up with the trees past the field. Cam paced back a few yards with his eyes glued on his target and then raced at the ball with determination. Just as he was ready to swing his foot back for the kick, he heard a voice shout from behind.

"Well, well, well. If it isn't the whale playing football all by himself. This is our field. Half-lives aren't allowed here. Get out!"

Cam didn't need to look. He knew that nasal, whining voice anywhere. Jason Morgan–the bully who lived in one of the better houses beyond the tree line.

A two-hundred-pound sack of disappointment slammed at Cam's

enthusiasm as he realized his practicing was now at an end. A screech from a nearby bird seemed to sympathize with his feelings. *Why did Jason have to come along and ruin everything?*

As Cam turned to look at Jason walking across the field, he wondered how such trash could look so good. Jason always seemed so fresh and clean with his neatly combed sandy blond hair and his lean body covered with clothes that looked like they'd just come from the store. To top it off, Jason's T-shirt even had the letter "J" on the pocket. *Over the top, man.*

In contrast, Cam felt like a giant sack of lumpy potatoes as he shoved his over-sized body into clothes from the second-hand store. At thirteen, his big build didn't always cooperate with what he wanted to do, and he was convinced he looked like a massive failure to others.

A recent talk Cam had with his Mom slid into his mind as though it was greased. He'd been complaining about his frustration with Jason.

"The guy acts like such a know-it-all," Cam said. "His Dad's a big shot in business, but Jason seldom sees him. Dad sees me more than his does, and mine doesn't even live here. Jason's mom always gives in to his demands. He hardly ever gets into trouble for the stuff he does. She makes excuses for him, and he's allowed to get away with just about anything."

"I feel sorry for Jason," Cam's Mom said as she poured water into the steaming pot on the stove. The spicy-sweet smell of spaghetti sauce filled the kitchen.

"What? Sorry for him?" Cam could hardly believe what he'd just heard. "He gets everything, Mom. I think he's lucky!"

"Oh no." She shook her head in disagreement. "Jason will be the one to lose in the end. He needs to experience the results of his behavior."

"Yeah, yeah, consequences. Right?" Cam grumbled. He'd heard it all before.

"You got it," his mom said as she stirred the spaghetti sauce. "Cam, kids who understand consequences are better prepared to deal with the world when they're adults. It doesn't sound like Jason's getting that lesson right now."

Still, Cam couldn't figure out what his mom was talking about. Jason was a giant suck; that's all.

Now, as he stood in the field, Cam turned to his nemesis, his empty fist clenched at his side. "I'm not going. This isn't your field. It's public property."

Jason advanced to Cam, and the two boys stood before one another in a glaring contest. Jason was so close Cam could feel his breath on his neck as the shorter boy tilted his head up to look into Cam's eyes.

"We're gonna practice for our showdown with the Trojans," Jason said, his fists planted on his hips, "and we don't need fat guts like you around to interfere. Get out, or we'll put you out."

Just then, Cam noticed the group of boys emerge from behind the trees. He should have known Jason's backup would be nearby. Otherwise, he doubted the guy would have the nerve to stand up to him alone. In silence, Jason's friends gathered behind him in a solid unit and listened to what was being said. Their scowls said to Cam, you heard him, get out!

Three of them, like Jason, were skinny with clean faces and stylish clothing. Two others were bigger, although not as chunky as Cam, nor as tall.

Were problems going to follow him around all day? Cam hadn't only come here to practice. He'd also hoped to get away from other problems and spend some time alone doing what he loved. Now everything was wrong—nothing was going right—nothing. The whole world felt like a freakish, twisted mess, with Cam stuck right in the middle. Everyone said it was his age, just a phase he was going through. Yeah right. Deep in his gut, he knew it was worse than that. Otherwise, why was he always in trouble? Why, all of a sudden, did his mom watch for all the things he did wrong?

'Clean your room. Pick up your mess. Do your homework; stop this; do that...'

As the group glared at him, Cam brought his thoughts back to what was happening here on the field. His stomach churned as he realized he was not going to win this one. A truck's motor rumbled in the distance, and kids on the playground equipment screamed in delight. Nearby a noisy squirrel chattered while birds twittered and fluttered from tree to tree. Yet these sights and sounds seemed to skim across the surface of Cam's mind as his attention focused on the gang before him. Now that Jason's slimy friends were there, the chance of maintaining his place on the field turned to zero. Still, he wasn't ready to give in.

"No. I'm not finished practicing." He glared at them.

Turning to his friends, Jason pointed at Cam and said, "Hey guys, Blimp wants to practice football." Looking at Cam, he laughed. "What team would want you representing them? You're a loser."

Anger flooded through Cam and prickled every nerve. He felt blood rush to his face and his breath became short gasps. His muscles took on a life of their own and stiffened, ready for action. His body tightened into a rigid board, all set for the attack.

"You're a misfit in the world." Jason jabbed his index finger into Cam's chest. His face took on a twisted look of contempt. "You walk around in your ratty clothes, trashing up the neighborhood. Our team doesn't need scum like you."

Cam's anger turned into boiling rage. "Yeah, well, you're the wimp who needs his friends to fight for him."

At that point, Cam looked over to the group of boys. He had no sooner turned his attention away from Jason when he felt a fist squarely pound his left ear, and a ringing echo engulfed his head.

As if on cue, the gang stepped back and surrounded the fighters while their shouts of "Go! Go! Go!" polluted the air.

Without thought, Cam swung and landed a good one on Jason's right cheek. Jason staggered back. Cam was just getting started. There was no stopping him as his fists repeatedly swung at Jason.

After Cam had landed several effective punches, someone grabbed his T-shirt from behind.

"Stop it." A voice sneered in his ear.

He stumbled as he was yanked back from Jason by unseen appendages pinning his arms behind him. He twisted to see what was happening and saw three of Jason's gang holding him. Without warning, a blow smashed the side of his head. Jason had free access at Cam as he struggled against the grip holding him but continued to suffer repeated blows to his face, chest, and stomach. Powerless, he fought to get free. Just then, one of the bigger boys stepped forward and shoved himself between Cam and Jason.

"Okay, cool it," the boy shouted above the screams of the other boys. "That's enough."

Jason, too angry to notice, or care, kept punching at Cam.

"Ouch," the bigger boy shouted as he got the last punch on the back of his head and fought to grasp Jason's fists in his own. "Stop it! That's enough." He looked at the other boys who pinned Cam's arms behind him. "Let him go!" Then he reached down and grabbed Cam's football from the ground. "You better get outta here, or I'll let them get you next time." He shoved the ball at Cam.

Snatching his ball from the boy, Cam stood rigid. Through clenched teeth, he screamed at Jason, "I'm gonna get you, you chicken head. When your thug pals aren't around to protect you, then I swear I'll do you maximum damage!"

As Cam stomped off the field, his resentment of living in government housing grew. Many times over the eight years his family had lived here, he'd felt as though he, and his people, were rabble that didn't belong anywhere. Lately, he saw football as a way out. It was just a glimmer, but maybe—you just never could tell.

His large, bulky build in the past had been an embarrassment to him. He'd endured constant ridicule from the other kids. Each barb felt like a link in a chain that locked him into this life of poverty. That was before he realized he could use his stocky build to his advantage. *I'll become a football player. Not just any football player either, I'll be famous. Then, if I'm good enough, I can go to college on a scholarship and get out of this place.*

None of that was going to come true if he couldn't get on the school's football team, and he needed to practice to do that. How was he going to get around Jason and his gang?

Chapter 2

Marcy

Cam heard the mocking voices trail behind him as he stomped from the field. If anyone from the neighborhood witnessed his shame, he didn't want to know about it. Humiliated, he kept his gaze on the ground, inches in front of his feet.

With each step, ants scrambled away in a haphazard pattern in their rush for survival. The trees in the woods where he headed showed off their bright new leaves to the world. Yet, Cam took no notice of the world around him.

His face and ears were on fire—his cheeks were the color of the tomatoes from last night's salad. Just one more problem with having red hair. He could never hide his embarrassment the way other people could. Cam felt sick to his stomach, his body shook, and he was sure his unsteady legs would give out at any moment. *Yeah, right, that'd be my luck to fall and bring myself even further shame.*

He was fed up with Jason's constant ridicule. For the last three years, they had been in the same class at school, but this year was the worst. "He just won't let up," he said to the dusty earth as he trudged through the woods toward the river. "*I feel like a hippo! And there's no one I can go to for help. I have to handle this problem myself, but how?*

'You're not fat,' his dad had told him. *'You're just husky like me. We've got big bones and muscles, that's all.'*

Cam thought maybe some of that was true, but it didn't stop his size from embarrassing him. And Jason's constant reminders didn't help. He also despised his blast of unruly red hair. Cam had thought about dyeing it or shaving his head, but then he figured he'd just give Jason more ammunition to taunt him.

And then there was his mom freaking out about his new friends. Max and Ruddy were okay—well, sort of. Deep in his heart, Cam knew what his mom was worried about. Both of them smoked and were trying to get him to join them. The first time he tried it, he had choked and coughed. The guys got a good laugh from that. Okay, okay, if he allowed himself to think about it, he knew they wanted to do a bit more than just smoke cigarettes. Like the time Ruddy had stolen some stuff from the store at the mall. And if he thought about it, he had to include the time when Max wanted to smash out cars' windows in the middle of the night. Plus, there was the time they'd come to his house with pot, *'funny cigarettes,'* his dad called them.

Yeah, I know these aren't the best things to do. Yet, the way Mom acted, you'd think I had joined a gang or something. There were worse kids than those guys, and a bit of pot wasn't going to kill anyone.

His mom was too old. She didn't understand. Anyway, the point was that Max and Ruddy liked him. They didn't give him a hard time about his clothes or size. They accepted him just the way he was. Couldn't his mom see that? At school, he had to put up with jerks like Jason. And, as if that wasn't enough, his bratty little sister was no joy either. She acted like the whole world should give in to her never-ending demands. Had he grown a "kick me" sign on his back?

Cam gave his head a shake, trying to get rid of the disturbing thoughts that dominated his brain. The soothing shade of the woods and the sound of the river beckoned to him. There he could be alone and calm down. The walk through the woods helped distract him from his frustration. The shade of the trees and gentle whispering breeze cooled his anger. He stepped through a line of bushes and saw the river and grassy shore calling to him.

At the river's edge, Cam yanked his T-shirt off, knelt and

dunked it in the water to wipe the blood and sweat from his face. Trickles of water ran down his hot neck and chest, and the refreshing coolness had a soothing effect he liked. He draped the wet shirt over his football on the grassy riverbank and lay down to use it as a pillow. The sun's warmth, the lapping ripples, and the soft spring grass drained the tension from his body.

The crack of a branch caused a lump in his throat. Every muscle in his body jumped to attention. Assuming the worst, Cam leapt to his feet and snatched his T-shirt. As he whirled around, he shoved the shirt over his head, not caring that it was inside out, and prepared himself for battle. His muscles relaxed as he watched Marcy step out into the sunshine.

A friend—a true friend! Marcy didn't see weight or wardrobe; she just saw her buddy since grade two when her family moved into the housing project. Since then, he felt her warmth and acceptance of him. They made each other laugh as she put humorous twists on things. They laughed together without feeling forced or out of place. Then, of course, her whooping laughter made everyone chuckle.

'I just feel happier when I'm with you,' she once told him. He thought it was a strange remark at the time—that is, it seemed weird until last week. That's when Lawrence, his other long-time good buddy, told him that Marcy had a "thing" for him.

Something akin to a wave of electricity rippled through Cam when he learned this, and his heart skipped a beat. After that, somehow, she looked different. Why hadn't he noticed how her long blond hair glistened in the sun? And her pleasing, petite figure made him blush.

"Hey, Cam, what're you doing?" As she neared, she squinted as though she could sense something was not right. "You don't look right. Are you okay?"

"Jason."

"Jason Morgan?" Marcy sputtered as she placed her fists on her hips. "Why, he's—he's just an intestinal disease."

"An obnoxious piece of vomit," Cam said with a chuckle. "He and his weasel teammates kicked me off the field because they wanted to use it for football practice." Cam shook his head. "I don't get it. Why do they need to practice there? They could use the school's field—it's in a lot better shape."

Marcy's laugh sounded like the howl of a whooping crane. The kids at school had begun to call her 'Whooper' because of it. She figured Jason had started the name she hated.

"I know why," she said to Cam and grinned. "One of the guys in my class said the coach told Jason and his gang that if they didn't pick up their grades and attend more practices, they'd never make next year's team. And would you believe it—just before this, Jason had been bragging to everyone how he was so valuable to the team that the coach couldn't possibly manage without him." Her eyes sparkled with glee.

"That's the best news I've heard in a very long time." Cam raised his arms like he scored a winning touchdown. "What goes around, comes around."

Cam knew the football season was still three months away, but it never ended for him. In his dreams, he saw himself negotiating around a linebacker from the opposing team. He zig-zagged through the other squad with nimble agility like they were wooden pegs and bolted to the end of the field. As he flashed beneath the goalpost, he threw his arms up to signal a successful touchdown as the ball went flying into the air.

"Cam. Cam." Marcy's voice penetrated his reverie, "Earth to Cam."

With regret, he pulled himself away from his daydream. It was such a cool dream.

"I have something else to tell you…"

Marcy's tone became more severe as the sparkle in her eyes blurred, and her smile diminished until it became a frown.

"I guess you haven't heard the latest."

She peered at Cam as if she hoped he might already have a clue what she was about to say. He merely returned a perplexed gaze.

"Jason's been threatening everybody with their life if they work with you on the science project."

Gone was the happiness of a moment ago. "What!" He felt like a boulder crashed into his gut. He opened his mouth to say something, but nothing came. Then a jolt of red-hot adrenaline pumped through his body in a gush. "No way."

For the last two weeks, Cam had been looking for a partner for his science project. It was the final assignment of the year. Yet, everyone had excuses as to why they couldn't work with him. Too bad Lawrence and Marcy weren't in his class because they wouldn't care about Jason's threats. He should have known Jason was behind it—he just should have known. "That piece of trash. Oh man, I hate that guy. I just gotta get him, Marcy—I just gotta."

"Can I help?" She held her fists out in front as if she were a boxer preparing for a fight. "I'll be your lookout, or I can pin him down."

"Great, Marcy, with your help, I'm sure to win."

"You better let me be there to help, or else."

"Or else what?"

"Or else…" She reached down to grab a handful of water. "I'll have to drown you." She threw a handful of water at Cam. Then she ran off towards home with a whoop, and Cam once more found himself laughing.

Chapter 3

The School Assignment

On his way home later, Cam passed the field where he'd been practicing football before Jason and his gang had shoved him out. Although the area was empty, an instant replay of his humiliation crowded his thoughts. He wondered if others had seen his shame, and he would face even more ridicule at school. Tension clenched his body and soured the pleasure he had enjoyed with Marcy.

As Cam burst into his house, he was relieved to see his mom wasn't home yet. The last thing he needed was for her to see his dirty, bloody T-shirt. In giant leaps, he flung himself up the stairs two at a time, and halfway up almost tripped on something. As he bent to pick it up, he grumbled, "What a stupid place to leave a doll."

Tara, his ten-year-old sister, leaned over the upstairs railing, "Give me my doll. I want her." she bellowed at the top of her lungs.

"What're you doing leaving it on the stairs then?"

Her angry, round, freckled face, planted on a skinny body, stared down at him. Dark red ponytails protruded from the sides of her head and seemed to emphasize her grouchiness.

He wasn't sure what he thought about his younger sister. At

times, she was okay, and then, he liked her. He wasn't ready to even think about loving her but liking seemed acceptable. Most of the time, though, she was a royal pain, always running to Mom for every little thing. He didn't even like her then, never mind love her.

"I only put her there for a minute 'cause I just wanted to get something," Tara said. "I was gonna take her downstairs with me."

"Tough luck because I'm not giving her back."

Just then, they heard a commotion from below, and Cam watched his mom stumble in the back door with an armload of groceries.

Tara began to yell, "You freak. I hate you." Then, even louder, "I'm gonna tell Mom on you!"

She scrambled down the stairs, shoved past him, and the doll as she whined out her complaints along the way. Cam squeezed the doll as hard as he could.

Tara barely took a breath between words. "Mom, Cam's being a brat. He won't give my doll back. I only left her there for a minute, and now he's keeping her from me."

Cam heard his mother's angry voice, "Don't you worry, little lady, I'll be dealing with him soon enough."

Then, Cam remembered that he didn't want his Mom seeing the condition of his T-shirt. Her tone and choice of words told him that he was already in some mysterious trouble. *Right. That fits the pattern of my life*. He dropped the doll back where he'd found it and bound up the stairs. At the same moment his mother's voice reached through space and caught him.

"Cameron Warner, come here!"

As he raced to his bedroom, he pulled the shirt off. His mother only called him "Cameron Warner" when she was angry. *Definitely in trouble*. He hollered back, "Coming, Mom." He stuffed the dirty shirt under his pillow in one swift movement and grabbed a less dirty one from the floor. As he shoved it over his head, he jogged for the stairs.

While his mom waited in the kitchen, Cam headed for the living room, threw himself into the easy-chair, and crossed his arms in a pout. *Why is she mad at me this time?* Was she upset because of the doll, his messy bedroom, his buddies, or maybe it was going to be a complete surprise.

His mother, a slim, pretty woman with dark auburn hair, stood before him. Her arms were crossed, and her face wore a look of coming trouble.

Not one of her good days. Maybe he could disappear under his chair.

"I wasn't gonna hurt her stupid doll," he said in a rush of words. "I was just bugging her." Forgetting that he had also left the doll on the stairs, he said, "Anyway, she left it on the stairs. I almost trip..."

Allison cut him off mid-sentence. "Your homeroom teacher called me at work today."

Confusion shoved across his mind. "He…he did?"

"You haven't been getting your assignments done."

Had he just walked into the middle of a mystery? He didn't know what was going on. Of course, he was doing his assignments so that he could make next year's football team. On that point, the coach was firm. Anyone wanting to play football had to do their schoolwork. What was the teacher telling her?

"That's not true," he yelled in frustration. "I've been getting my work done."

"Your science project?"

Dejected, he slumped in his chair. Mr. Abernathy, his science teacher, wasn't being fair. More calmly, he explained to his Mom what Marcy told him when they were by the river.

Allison's face softened in sympathy. "Oh, Cam," she said tenderly. Then her tone once more became firm. "Then I guess you'll have to do it alone."

"Yeah, I know," he said. "I'll go on Sunday."

"I don't think so." All the anger left her voice, but she was still firm. "Sorry, Cam, I know you're disappointed, but I want you to do it first thing tomorrow morning."

As he started to protest, she held up her hand, palm forward to silence him until she finished.

"It's already overdue, and you haven't even started. So, if it's not done by noon tomorrow, you'll be grounded. Now, would you please come and help with supper."

"That's not fair!" Cam said in bitter defeat. "How come I always have to help? How come my fat-faced little sister never has to do anything?" Of course, he only said things like this when he forgot about the times when it was Tara's turn to help with the dishes or meals.

The frustration turned to pleading and begging. "I promise I'll do the experiment on Sunday. Honest. Dad's coming tomorrow. Come on, Mom, can't it wait just a little? I'll go on Sunday when I come home from Dad's. Pleeease?"

Spending time with his father was his favorite activity. His parents had divorced almost six years ago, and he always looked forward to spending alternate weekends with his Dad. He figured he would have gone every weekend if he could, except Tara had to have her turn, and his parents both said they fought too much to go together. His mother had to give in. She just had to.

Allison was relentless. "That's enough! If I hear another word, you'll be grounded for the whole weekend. If you haven't gone to the river for the water by noon tomorrow, you will force me to call your father and tell him you can't make it. Now, either get busy helping me or put your pajamas on. Which is it going to be?"

He thundered toward the kitchen in defeat. "Man, I hate this place. I hate where we live, I hate my life, and I hate her." He stabbed a finger toward his sister, who was sitting on the bottom stair clutching her doll and smirking.

Chapter 4

Breem

The sun had just broken free of the horizon on this warm May morning, and the day promised to be a beauty. A robin called out to the world from a nearby tree and invited all to join him in this lovely start on the day. All the more reason to get his task done quickly. That way, Cam could enjoy this great weather with his dad.

Since he was working harder to keep his schoolwork up to date, he had begun to enjoy the new things, aside from discovering what he could do when motivated. Not this morning. Now bad-tempered Cam wondered if it was worth the effort. On second thought, football made it worth it. "Let's get this over with."

As Cam trudged across the grass toward his bike that leaned against the back fence, his shoulders slumped, his hands, stuffed deep into his pockets. Angry, he kicked at the grass, and a spray of water splattered in the air before him. "Just my luck; it rained last night. Now, my new runners will get ruined."

He stopped sudden-like, as though he'd just slammed into a wall. A bright and hopeful smile lit his face. "*Hey…*" He held up a finger to the sky. "*I'll use the water from these leaves for my project. Then I won't have to go all the way to the marsh. No one will know, after all, water's water. Right? If this works, I can go with Dad.*"

He pulled a plastic pill vial from his pocket and began gathering rainwater from the broad dandelion leaves and grass. When the vile was half-full, he carried it to his room. At times like these, he was grateful for the microscope his dad had given him for his birthday. With caution, he placed a few drops of the liquid on the glass slide and peered at them through the lens.

In the magnified water droplet, there was the strangest looking germ he had ever seen. The weird microbe stood on two legs in a puddle of water.

Cam felt a jolt run through his body as if lightning struck him. He could see a cartoon eye staring up the microscope into his eye.

At the same moment, he was positive he heard a tiny voice squeak, "Fantastic, I did it!"

A large blue flash filled his bedroom. Micro-seconds later, a much larger version of the microbe sat on his dresser.

Stunned, Cam realized it wasn't his imagination. He could see the creature from the other end of the microscope here in his room. To make things stranger, it was a cartoon character.

Cam felt like someone threw a bowling ball right through the middle of his brain and sent the pins spinning in different directions. Pulling things back to where they belonged was tricky. Cam rubbed his eyes, convinced that when he looked again, everything would be back to normal. Seconds later, he peered through his fingers. The cartoon creature still sat on the dresser, appearing pleased with itself.

His mind raced with questions. *What's going on? Who or what is that thing? What's it doing here in my bedroom? Is it friendly?*

As though covered with grease, the being slid off the dresser and scanned the room. It looked almost as tall as Cam, but at least double his size around—Cam felt skinny beside this…ah…guy? Most of the creature's height came from his sizeable blue body. The small purple vest that didn't cover his entire chest further emphasized his size.

The creature's short stubby legs barely kept his round tummy from scrapping the ground. His arms, on the other hand, were skinny and long. When held downward, they came to his knees.

The strange being's head was quite large with a short, pig-like nose. His face looked like a cross between a pig and a wrinkled dog. Sagging creases competed with one another for space on his face. His warm, friendly eyes were enormous green teardrops, capped by thick lashes. Wild, stubborn-looking blue fur crowned the creature's head. It reminded Cam of his own hair. It, too, had a will of its own.

Cam inched away until the back of his legs bumped into his bed, and he plopped down. His mouth opened to say something, but he couldn't make a sound and snapped it shut. His stomach tightened. His breathing shortened.

Fear and aggression seized him. For all he knew, this strange beast might be dangerous. Its size alone sent a cringe down his spine.

"What's happening?" He stood in one quick jerk, ready for action. "Who are you? Where'd you come from?"

"This is terrific, the best!" The creature's low voice sounded as though it came through a hollow tube.

"What're you talking about? Who are you? What are you doing here?" Cam asked.

The creature stood quietly, examining everything in his midst with his big, happy smile, oblivious of the questions Cam flung at him.

Curiosity satisfied, the creature turned to greet his host. "Hi there, I'm Breem! Who are you?"

Cam wasn't impressed with how this guy just took charge. After all, this was his room and his world, so he should be the one in control. "I'm not answering any of your questions until you answer some of mine."

Undeterred by Cam's grouchiness, the creature agreed. "Okay, I'll go first—if you insist. My name's Breem, and I come from Worpple."

"From where?"

"Worpple, it's a parallel world to yours. Okay, it's actually a parallel dimension, to be exact. I'm here on a school assignment."

Cam had learned about dimensions in science. The teacher told the class about a guy named Carl Sagan, who talked about a make-believe place called "Flatland," where all the people were only two dimensions, length, and width, but had no height. Cam was aware he lived in a three-dimensional world with width, length, and height. Still, he was having a hard time imagining a cartoon dimension.

"Why did you come to my world?" Cam asked, losing some of his defensiveness. "Why didn't you go to another one?"

"That's easy." Breem grinned "Because your yard has an opening between our dimensions."

Fascinating. Maybe this guy is all right, after all. He looks strange, but he isn't threatening in any way. "You're from another dimension? That's excellent. And you came here for a school assignment? I don't believe it. I don't even want to go to the swamp for a school project, let alone to another dimension."

"You don't?" Breem looked at Cam in confusion. "I love school." Then his face grew thoughtful as he cradled his chin in his hand. "Then again, I love life and learning. Oh yeah, then there's meeting new people." He paused. "Of course, I also love going to new places and doing new things. Okay," Breem shrugged, looking at Cam, "I guess I just love adventure. I never miss an opportunity to explore. You never know what might be waiting there."

Questions once more flooded Cam's mind. "How'd you get here? What's it like in Worpple? Does everyone look like you?"

"Hold on!" Breem laughed and paused a moment to answer Cam's questions. "How about coming back with me? Then you could find out for yourself."

"By the way," Breem added, "do you happen to have a towel so I can dry myself? I seem to be creating a small river here in your room."

Cam was so excited that he couldn't think straight. He handed Breem a T-shirt that decorated his floor. "Here, use this."

His new friend's invitation was sinking into his brain, "Could I really come with you? That would be awesome! How can I do that? I mean, you were so small before. How'd you get like that?"

Breem dried himself with the T-shirt. "Sure, you can come. My school assignment is to find a life-form from this world and bring it back with me. I was originally thinking of a caterpillar or a bug, but you can be my life-form if you want."

As Cam grew more and more excited, he started to do a crazy dance around the room. It wasn't every day that someone asked you if you could be their life-form. *Imagine, I can visit another world!* He could almost tap dance on the ceiling as all thoughts of danger vanished, and he decided he liked the cheerful, friendly creature after all.

"Wow, that's great! Oh yeah, my name's Cam. So, do I have to get small like you were? Why were you so small?"

"Well, the only way we can enter your world is through squishers," Bream said.

"What's a squisher?"

"Oh, I forgot." Breem chuckled, "You don't know that word. They are tiny openings between our dimensions that are hard to squeeze through. There are only a couple of these squishers around. One happens to be in your yard. And if you want to come into my world, I'll have to shrink you."

Cam pulled back. Shrink him? How would that feel? Would it hurt? What if, after Breem shrank him, he still didn't fit through the opening? And worst of all, what if Breem couldn't get him back to his regular size again?

"Maybe this isn't such a good idea after all," he said in a whispered croak as he stared down at the floor.

As if able to read Cam's mind Breem assured him. "Don't worry. You won't feel a thing. I've been in your world lots of times." He paused. "Well, maybe not exactly lots, more like three times. Still, if it were painful, I wouldn't be here right now. Nothing can go wrong, I promise. Come on, let's go."

Breem's easygoing manner and friendly approach assured Cam he was in no danger. He led his new buddy to where Cam had collected the water earlier.

Breem began searching the ground. "Now, where did I leave my marker?" he asked. "Can you remember exactly where you found me?"

"No clue. I think it was over there, closer to the end of the yard." Pointing, Cam walked to the fence. "Somewhere near these dandelions. That leaves us an area of about this much." He circled his arms around the appropriate area. "What're we looking for? What kind of marker did you leave?"

"It's a large, bright red stone, but it's tiny now. It's probably not much bigger than a dot."

"Hey, I'll get my magnifying glass," he said as he ran toward the house. "Don't worry; we'll find it."

Cam and Breem crawled around on the wet ground for the next ten minutes, looking for the marker. Cam reached out his hand to spread apart the leaves and grass as he peered through his magnifying glass. At last, Breem gave a whooping cry as he located the red stone.

Just then, Cam stopped and threw his hands up in the air. "Oh, no! I can't go with you," he said in exasperation. "I want to go with Dad this afternoon, but if I don't get my school assignment done, Mom will ground me for the whole weekend."

"What's the assignment?"

"Oh, I'm supposed to go to the marsh and get some water to examine for micro-organisms. I was trying to cheat and use rainwater when I found you."

"Then you can still come! We have lots of marshes in Worpple, and I guarantee you'll be home in plenty of time to go with your father."

"You promise I'll be back in time?"

Holding his right hand up to the sky, Breem assured him. "I promise."

"Aalll riiigght! Let's go."

"Okay, Cam, just squat yourself down here," Breem said, "right by the marker. Get as close to it as you can, and I'll squeeze in right next to you."

After they were in position, Breem asked, "Are you ready? Here we go."

Breem put his arm around Cam's shoulders, reached inside his vest, and pushed a button near the top. A moment later, a bright blue ray surrounded them. In a way he couldn't understand, Cam watched himself and Breem become smaller and smaller.

"Fantastic!" Cam shouted. Breem had been right. There was no pain. Instead, he felt as though he was on a fast carnival ride. His stomach pitched and rolled as he shrank.

Soon they were the right size to fit through the squisher. Cam looked down to find a bright red rock separating them. Confidently, Breem stepped around the boulder and grabbed what appeared to be invisible air. If Cam didn't know an opening existed, he would have missed the fuzzy line his friend reached toward. As the seam widened, it looked as though a sheer curtain from nowhere spread apart. Holding the gap open, Breem instructed Cam to crawl through to the other side. Cam agreed the squisher was well named as he had to squeeze to get through. Next, he watched as a red rock came through the opening and dropped on the ground by him. Then Breem squirmed his ample bottom through the dimensional doorway.

Chapter 5

Worpple

As soon as they were both in Worpple, Breem grabbed a firm hold of Cam's shoulder, pushed the vest-button, and, like a jack-in-the-box, they sprang back to their usual sizes. Cam had a swoosh feeling in his gut as though his stomach had stayed behind and was racing to catch up.

Cam saw a charming, cartoon meadow filled with strange flowers and plants as he looked around. He stared in fascination at the alien world that encircled him. Some nearby flowers looked like glass. He could see through the petals and into the center where their brightly colored stamens invited insects to sip their nectar. Others looked like bells ready to ring, while still others appeared to be dancing ballerinas.

As if to support this illusion, beautiful music flowed across the meadow toward Cam as he took in the scene. *That's odd. I can't see any musical instruments or singers. There isn't even a boom box lying in the purple grass.*

He strained to listen and was sure he heard a woman sing out to him.

"Cam, welcome to the 'Magical-Musical Garden,'" the sweet voice sang.

Breem beamed. "So, what do you think? Pretty terrific, huh?"

"That music, where's it coming from?" Cam asked in confused amazement. "And how did they know I was going to be with you?"

"No one knew you were coming. Well, not exactly," Breem said, his large green eyes twinkled merrily. "This is the Magical-Musical Garden, and the music is coming from the plants around you. Welcome, Cam!"

From the plants? Had he heard, right? "But plants can't play music."

"The plants in this garden can," Breem said. "If you listen carefully, you'll notice that each plant sounds like a different instrument."

Cam paused to soak up this new experience. "Wow! I wish we had gardens like this. But I still don't get it. The voice is singing out my name. How does the singer know who I am, or that I was coming?"

"That's the magical part. I'll explain, but remember, it's going to seem pretty strange to you and not at all what you're used to."

"Okay."

"Do you see that big blue plant in the middle of the garden?"

Breem pointed and waited until Cam looked in the right direction.

"That's Julie. She's special here in Worpple. Come closer, and I'll introduce you. Be careful where you walk. Don't step on any plants."

Breem led Cam down a twisting orange path through the purple grass toward what appeared to be a blue cartoon flower. As he drew near, Cam gasped in surprise. "What's that?"

There was a blue, comic-strip woman—almost. Looking closer, he saw that she was, indeed, a large plant growing from the ground.

She stood about three feet tall with a female body and arms created from long slender leaves. Her head looked like a bird with a flower for a hat.

Cam had only been in Worpple a few minutes and already had gone from wonder to wonder. It was so different from his world—like a carnival sideshow filled with alien creatures. Still, the friendly atmosphere all around put him at ease.

"This is an amazing garden," he told Breem. Suddenly, he jumped and spun around. He was sure he heard a beautiful voice thanking him. Stranger still, the words were in his head—not in his ears.

As he spun to locate the source of the voice, he looked at Breem. His new friend doubled over in spasms of laughter. Cam wasn't sure he appreciated being a source of a joke. He had enough of that at home. "Hey man, don't fall over yourself. I'm glad you're enjoying this so much."

"Sorry, it's just so funny," Breem worked to straighten his face and dab his eyes. Once he gained control of himself, he explained. "Julie's a telepath. She can't speak to you like most people; instead, she talks in your mind. She can also read your thinking. That's how she knew your name."

Cam felt as though an ice cube was creeping down the back of his neck. If Julie could read his thoughts, would she become angry if he gave his attention to the wrong thing? His first instinct was to protect his opinions, but how? Then, as if being told, he realized that everyone was so warm and friendly that nothing terrible would happen to him. He would have to trust his instincts and go with the experience.

"You mean the beautiful singing voice I heard was hers?" Turning to Julie, he said, "You're too cool. It's a shame we can't take you back to Earth with us. You'd make a killing."

Julie covered her beak with her leaf-hand, giggled, and pretended to be upset.

She said, "I do not want to kill anyone."

When she spoke, she had the lilting singsong accent of a soft-spoken East Indian woman he knew.

He felt his face and ears redden. "Oh no! I didn't mean that." Then he realized Julie was teasing him. "Yeah, right." He laughed along with Julie.

Breem said, "Another magical part of this garden is that it's one of two places where there's a squisher to your world. To go through the opening, we need Julie's approval. She's kind of like the guard. So, you see, Julie knew I was coming back with someone. She just didn't know it would be you."

"That's amazing."

"We should get going. I want to show you around our world. Come on."

Julie wished Cam a pleasant visit as they turned to leave.

"See you later, Julie." Breem and Cam waved as they left the garden.

"Where are we going now?" Cam asked as they followed a path through the woods that surrounded the Magical-Musical Garden.

"I want to show you my school and then maybe some other places."

"Is your school far from here?"

"No, not at all—at least it's not as far as the Moving Forest."

"Moving Forest? That's a weird name for a forest. Does it move all the time?"

"Not exactly." Breem pushed some overhanging branches out of their way. Their path narrowed. Cam followed in single file, which made conversation difficult for a while.

Chapter 6

Magic

On the other side of the Moving Forest, a great distance from Julie's garden, stood a tumbled-down shack. It may have been a friendly cottage at one time. Perhaps it had housed a happy family or a cheerful forest ranger. Now, bright sunlight struggled through a thick filter of forest, vines, and trees. Over-grown bushes and boarded-up windows allowed dim light to seep into the gloomy interior. There, long threatening shadows cast by the fireplace's flickering flames squirmed across the walls as if in agony. In the grim darkness, an arm reached out to a large kettle hanging above the fire as swirls of steam curled into the air.

A grumpy voice rumbled in anger. "I'll show them for forcing me to live in exile. Well, they won't ignore me much longer. Just because I'm so big doesn't give them the right to reject me. They will pay attention real soon. Then, everyone is going to give me respect."
"Garbon, luxis, forte, snee," The creature's deep voice filled the room as it repeated the chant. A dark and shadowy hand reached out of the gloom and dropped strange ingredients into the boiling pot. "Borbol, dilgar, rosis, gnee."

The conjurer uttered a great sigh that cut through the shadowy room, and then he sat back waiting for something to happen. Maybe there would be a massive puff of smoke and a genie or something equally magical would appear. He wasn't sure what to expect because the book he had gotten the spell from didn't say what would happen after performing the ritual. As he waited, a worm of fear began in his stomach and worked its way up toward his heart. Foreboding and dread filled him.

"That's strange..." The creature moaned. "I feel worse than ever. I thought I was supposed to feel better. What do I do now?"

Chapter 7

The Madra Stone

Cam followed Breem through the forest on an orange path wide enough for only one person. He was fascinated by the strange plants that grew on both sides of the trail. Some trees looked like giant spirals that reached up, up into the sky. He figured they would be easy to climb, but he didn't take the time to find out. Some trees took the shape of massive ice cream cones. Another looked like a regular tree on his world, but those made him nervous when its branches seemed to reach out at him as he passed. He gave that tree lots of room and scurried by, although Breem didn't seem to be concerned at all. On either side of the path, the same sparkling purple grass Cam had seen in the Musical Magical Garden covered the ground. Sprinkled here and there were brilliant turquoise and orange flowers.

As they walked, Breem explained about the opening to his world. "We've known about the openings to your world for a long time but didn't start going there until a few years before I was born."

"How come?" Cam tore his attention away from the strange scenery.

"Well, there was a large debate going on about it. Some of our people wanted to learn about your technology, and others were afraid of it. They didn't want to take any chances of contact at all. And others thought going to your world would change us too much."

"Why would anyone be afraid? We're nice people."

"Your technology is much farther advanced than ours, and most people are friendly, but in other ways, we're more advanced than you."

"Huh? How are you more advanced? I don't see any buildings, and here we are walking to your school. I don't see where this world has anything better than mine."

"Well," Breem said, "we're ahead of you in the area of relationships. We don't have any pollution, and we've never had a war, at least not that I know of."

Cam hung his head and stared at the ground. He had to admit his world did have a lot of wars. Then a thought came to him. "You're right. We do have wars—too many. But those same wars brought a lot of our technology."

He stared at the ground and walked as he remembered the lesson from his history course. In his mind, he saw Mr. Gilbert facing the class, his hands stuffed deep into his pockets. Light from the window reflected off the top of his bald head as he spoke. He was a short man with bowed legs that caused him to sway as he paced in front of the class.

"Why do we study history?" The teacher's rumbling voice filled the room. "Well," he answered his own question, "humans have a habit of repeating the same errors over and over. By studying the past, we can learn from history's mistakes and hopefully not make them again."

Mr. Gilbert stopped and studied the class as though making sure everyone was listening. "We study history," he resumed his pacing, "so we know how and why something happened and because it is interesting to see how things have evolved. The teacher stopped and posed a few questions to the class. "Why did the communists come into power in the Soviet Union? How come we've had two world wars? How does that relate to the development of the world?" The teacher leaned one hip against the edge of his desk and folded his arms across his chest.

"Did you know that during the second world war, we advanced farther with technology than we would have done if there had been no war? For example, during World War II, airplanes went from double-winged, puttering beasts, called biplanes, to those that went faster and farther in a fraction of the time.

"And," he held up a finger for emphasis, "did you know that the computer was brought into regular use because of the Second World War? Television and advanced forms of communication were also a result of wars. At least, the war brought them faster."

Cam shared these memories with Breem.

"Is that right?" his friend asked in surprise. "Then I guess we're sort of cheating. We are getting the technology without having to go through any wars."

"I think you coming to learn from my world is great."

"Yeah?" Breem's face brightened into a warm smile as he stepped over a tree root. "I'm glad you approve. I wasn't sure how you'd react if I told you. We are, after all, also learning from the mistakes of your history," he said with a chuckle. "Although, I suppose we'll make some of our own."

"I love it. I wonder what the guys back home would say if they knew? I won't tell them though. They'd never believe me. Anytime you want help when you're in my world, just come to me. I'd be happy to do whatever I can for you."

"Thanks, Cam, I'll remember that."

Cam examined the sparkling blades of purple grass as Breem continued.

"Now we make regular trips to your world to learn. We're bringing the computer over here and are discussing transportation options."

What about transportation would people need to discuss? "How come you're discussing that?" A bird in a nearby tree warbled as if in reaction to Cam's confusion.

"Well, we want to pick something safe for the environment, and we're considering our other options. Should we restrict it to public transportation for everyone's use or private cars? Cars sure have brought one big mess for your world. Anyway, we don't know what we are going to do yet."

As they talked, Cam continued to soak up the strange scenery. One tree caught his attention. Not much taller than an apple tree, two bright green trunks twisted together in an eternal embrace. Yet, it was the leaves that had him engrossed. They looked like enormous, orange balls of fluff. While he watched, one leaf broke away and glided to the ground. As it floated, it danced a smooth ballet on its way to the forest floor.

"These plants and trees, I've never seen anything like them. What a strange tree. What's it called?"

"That's an umbrella tree. The person to ask about the plants and animals around here is my best friend, Dwinda. She knows all about nature. I'll take you to meet her later."

Cam stooped to pick up a few of the large fluffy leaf-seeds. He was struck by how soft and light they were. As he held a leaf up to the sun, it seemed to sparkle like a jewel. His eye caught a flash of light from among the feathery leaves on the ground. At first, he had a hard time identifying if the glitter was from the jewel-like leaves or from something else on the ground. Reaching out to see, he discovered a magnificent stone, unlike anything he had ever seen before. As he held it in his hand, it began to glow as if it possessed a life of its own.

The stone's primary color was a vibrant, royal purple, yet swimming within the stone were swirls of color. Green, turquoise, and orange looked like a miniature aurora borealis happening within the stone. The pebble fit perfectly into the hollow of Cam's palm and felt like the ones from his world that had a smooth sand-washed finish. Except, this one emitted a pulsating throb of warmth as if it had been sitting in a hot place.

"Wow! What's this?"

Breem toddled over on short legs and peered into Cam's hand. In a muted tone of awe, he whispered, "I don't know."

They stood transfixed, staring at the stone as the swirling colors transformed into pink, yellow, and blue.

"Let's take it to school and ask Mr. Iber, my teacher," Breem whispered as though apprehensive about breaking the hushed quiet. "He might know something about it."

Cam reached for a handful of the silky umbrella leaves and wrapped the stone in them. Then, as if he were handling a precious gem, he placed the bundle deep into his front pocket. Again, the pair started for the school, but now he walked more carefully. He didn't want to disturb his remarkable discovery.

As they walked, Cam thought about what Breem had said about living in a world with no wars. The thought once more made him feel he was totally safe in this strange new land.

Chapter 8

School

It was hard to see the school from a distance. The low building blended into the environment of the forest. Cam saw no walls as they neared the strange structure, and the roof was entirely overgrown with plant-life. Vine-covered pillars held up the living roof.

"What kind of place is this? There aren't any walls. What do you do when it rains?"

"Well, the walls are tucked up into the roof," explained Breem. "They're made of a see-through material that rolls down. We don't worry about it much because there are so many trees surrounding the area that we're quite protected from the weather."

As he grew nearer, Cam saw a small group of bizarre-looking aliens sitting on the floor in a semicircle. In front of them was a creature he couldn't believe was a teacher. The blue instructor had the head of a dog, complete with floppy ears. Where one would expect to find arms, his round body had three octopus-like tentacles on each side. Cam couldn't help thinking of the number of times his mother said that she could use another pair of hands.

A dark pink character that looked like a dolphin with a skirted body sat close to the teacher. Two of Breem's classmates had flat heads with eyes that made them look half-asleep. Then there was a thin purple creature with pointed head, nose, and ears. So varied were the classmates that Cam stood and stared, his mind racing with curiosity and intrigue.

Counters and cupboards filled with equipment stood where the walls generally stood. At least that part looked like a regular school. Three computers sat on one shelf; another worktop held lab equipment where more strange beings were busy working.

"Excuse me." Breem called to his classmates. "Everyone, this is Cam. He's visiting from the Earth dimension." To Cam, he said, "This is Mr. Iber, our teacher."

The creature with the blue dog-head spoke, and the room was filled with the sound of a howling wolf. *What's that?* Cam whirled around to find the source of the noise.

"Welcome to our classroom," the wolf voice said. Cam realized it was coming from Mr. Iber. Before he could collect himself and respond, a group of classmates crowded around him. Some just wanted to touch him. Others had an endless list of questions.

"What kind of house do you live in?"

"What do you do there?"

"What do you eat?"

"How many friends do you have?"

"Does everyone look like you?"

Swamped though he was by these curious creatures, he was enjoying himself. "One at a time, please." He laughed. "I'm from Earth, and I live in a house. Mostly I go to school, spend time with my friends, and practice football." Cam paused to take a breath. "This is a weird school. How come you don't have any desks?"

A couple of students started to giggle. "We do," a few others said.

Walking to a counter nearby, Mr. Iber shouted for everyone to step back. In a flurry, the group scampered to the side of the room. At the same time, Cam felt as though a line of rope was wrapped around his waist as he was dragged off the floor.

He turned his head to find out what was happening. A thin purple pupil had enclosed him in tentacles and was yanking him from the middle of the room. He wasn't sure he appreciated being jerked off the floor like that. It would have been as effective and a whole lot nicer to allow him to move on his own. Still, he kept his temper and told himself the creature was only trying to help.

Once everyone was lined up around the side of the room, Mr. Iber pushed a button, and the whole floor seemed to turn upside-down. Desks and chairs materialized out of the ground.

Cam couldn't figure out how this strange world operated. "But why don't you use them?"

Breem explained. "We only use them when we're here for a long time. Usually, we aren't here long enough."

Mr. Iber's wolfish voice continued. "Our students do most of their learning testing their thoughts out in the world or at home on their computers. They only come to school long enough to share their discoveries or talk with a teacher about a specific area of interest. Plus, this way, the desks last longer."

Cam was dumbfounded. "You mean no one has to stay here all day if they don't want to? Now, this is my kind of school."

As he began to imagine a life without constant school attendance, Mr. Iber said, "We do have strict requirements, Cam. Usually, the assignments are individualized according to various factors. We consider the ages of the students, the interest levels, and the difficulty of their project. It's up to the students how they accomplish their tasks. If they run across difficulties, they're welcome to come to school for guidance. But we encourage our students to find their own answers as much as they are able. We don't have your large internet, so, at the end of each day, the other teachers and I share the discoveries and learning from that day through the computer with the students who weren't here."

Turning to Breem, Mr. Iber said, "You've done an excellent job on your project—you should be very pleased, Breem."

"Thanks. I'm more than pleased. I'm thrilled!" Breem's hollow voice said, "I've been to the other dimension before but have never communicated with the people there. Having Cam here is worth all the work." Breem patted his new pal on the back as if he were a long-lost buddy.

To Mr. Iber, Breem said, "Oh, I almost forgot, on our way here, Cam found an unusual stone."

In a flash, Cam yanked the bundle from his pocket, plucked the stone from the soft leaves, and held it out for the teacher's inspection. "Do you know what it is?" Breem asked his teacher.

"Oh my!" Mr. Iber exclaimed as he peered into Cam's extended hand. His usual wolf voice turned into a full howl of excitement. "I've seen pictures of these in books, but never in real life. I believe this is a Madra Stone."

"A what?" Cam asked through the heads of many students gathered around to catch a glimpse.

"Students, students," Mr. Iber shouted. "Stop shoving. Form a line, and each of you may have a good look, then give this poor boy some space. And no touching." Mr. Iber said with emphasis.

Cam realized that if the teacher had never seen a stone like this in his life, then here was a rare opportunity for the students to learn. He held out his hand with the pebble snuggled in his palm so that all the students could see. Again, it shone a royal purple. Various colors deep within swirled, changed, and then altered the colors, and the twisting began again. Eventually, the students returned to the desks after having a fascinated look. Their many oohs and ahs testified to their fascination with this wondrous object.

While the students were examining the stone, Mr. Iber told Cam, Breem, and the class what he knew. "From what I remember, the Madra Stone holds great magical powers. But this magic is meant only for the one who finds it. A Madra Stone will not work for anyone other than the one for whom it is intended." Pausing to look down at the stone, the teacher continued, "See how it glows in your hand right now, Cam?"

Cam glanced at the stone and nodded.

"Now, give the stone to Breem, and see what happens."

The second the stone touched Breem's hand, the stone's colors flickered out as if blowing out a match. It looked like an ordinary pebble one might find on a beach. Mr. Iber plucked it from Breem's palm and held it up for the class to see that the colors had blinked out like a light turned off. Yet as soon as Mr. Iber placed it back in Cam's hand, it sprang to colorful life again. Cam, too, held the stone up to show the difference to the class.

"That stone's yours alone," Mr. Iber said. "It won't work for anyone else. What's more, it will only continue to work its magic as long as it's needed. When you've accomplished the task the stone is here to help you with, it will revert to an ordinary stone. The magic in it is all yours. No one can steal it from you or use it against you."

Cam felt a jumble of emotions as he re-wrapped the stone and placed it back in his pocket. His brain felt like the clothes in his drawer, all confused and tossed around. The weight of responsibility was like a stone that filled his stomach with butterflies. What did it mean? Was he going to have to do something weird or essential? While a part of him was amazed to have the Madra Stone, he had mixed feelings of pride, pleasure, and nervousness at having been chosen.

Lost in these thoughts, the screech of a bird and someone running in the woods startled him back to reality. All eyes turned in the direction of the clamor and watched as a bright green female creature raced toward the school. She was yelling and waving her arms, clearly troubled.

Chapter 9

Dwinda

"Dwinda!" Breem exclaimed when he saw his friend rushing toward him with fear all over her face. Alarmed, he hurried to meet her, followed closely by everyone else.

Dwinda. That's Breem's best friend. She's the one who knows the name of all the plants and animals. As Cam watched the strange creature approach, he gave his head a shake. He thought he was getting used to this world of cartoon characters, but this creature really pushed the limit. Dwinda's bright green body enhanced her soft, blue eyes. She was a little shorter than Breem, but the point at the top of her head almost erased the difference. She almost reminded him of an ant. Her body was two round balls joined in the middle. Her human-like arms were attached by webbing, giving the effect that she wore a cape.

"Dwinda, what is it?" Breem cried in alarm. "I've never seen you this upset before. What happened?"

"Julie came to see me…" She panted. "…a few minutes ago." Gasping for breath, she reached down and grasped her knees. "She told me you were—here with Cam," she finally managed to say. She took some deep breaths, then straightened up and looked around. She spotted Cam, the only one there who was not a cartoon. Neglecting to introduce herself, she said, "I'm sorry, Cam, I didn't mean to be rude and interrupt your visit, but I'm anxious."

If he were to close his eyes and forget her appearance, Dwinda almost sounded like one of the girls in his class. This girl was always pleasant to him. He liked to talk to her.

"Don't worry," he said without hesitation. "I'm happy to help if I can. What's going on?"

"Julie told me a terrible thing has happened." Dwinda, now breathing almost normally, directed her next comments to everyone. "Somehow, malicious evil has entered our world."

"What are you talking about?" Mr. Iber asked in concern, the students crowding around him gasped.

"Julie was only able to pick up a weak signal over by the Moving Forest."

Breem stammered and wrapped his arms around himself, "But why, who, how did it happen?"

As she responded, Dwinda moved to get the sun out of her eyes and directed her answer to Breem. "The signal was too weak for Julie to tell us much. She said it seemed to come from the far side of the Moving Forest. She didn't know what it was but said something evil, and evil is growing in our world."

Once more, Cam's brain was in a muddle. "Excuse me, I'm confused. How can that flower-woman come here to warn Dwinda?"

Breem explained in a rush because he wanted to get back to Dwinda, "As I mentioned before, Julie's telepathic, so she can tell when things go wrong. If she senses problems, she can appear as a hologram to warn us." Breem paused and then added, "But, I don't ever remember her telling us anything this serious." He turned back to Dwinda.

"Unfortunately, there's a limit to her abilities," Mr. Iber said, continuing where Breem left off. "If the distance is too great, she can't pick up anything."

"At least she was able to get enough information to warn us," Dwinda said. "In the past, she's had suggestions about what we can do. This time she's almost as lost as we are."

"Almost!" Breem shouted. "What else did she say?" he asked.

"I really didn't want to tell you this part, Breem," Dwinda said. "Julie thinks you and I should find out what's happening. If we haven't found an answer by the time we reach the Moving Forest, then we might have to go to Zarlock. He should have some ideas."

"Did you say Zarlock?" Breem asked. "Wow! Now that's an amazing trip!" Then noticing the scowl on Dwinda's face, he said, "I know he lives far away, but it's still a great adventure getting there."

"Breem, this is hardly the time to be thinking of adventure," Dwinda said. "Anyway, I said we *might* go to Zarlock *if* we can't figure out what's causing the trouble."

Cam didn't completely understand everything, but he realized the situation was dire. Yet, he couldn't stop himself from asking, "Who or what is this Zarlock guy?"

Everyone turned to stare at Cam as though being directed by a choirmaster. As if to punctuate the group's astonishment, the noise of a small animal scurrying through the woods could be heard. "He doesn't know who Zarlock is," a young voice said from among the students.

Mr. Iber turned to Cam and explained. "He's a wise person who's been chosen by the inhabitants of Worpple. He or she is then given the title of 'The Zarlock.' It's a permanent role, and we must be careful when choosing the person for the position. We must select someone who is wise, kind, and has a broad knowledge base. We must also be cautious about choosing someone who will have an unlimited vision, trustworthiness, and life experience. It also helps if he or she has a sixth sense."

"Whenever there are problems, we can go to Zarlock for help," Dwinda said. "We usually only go when the trouble is serious because it's such a long and difficult journey. Zarlock can't come to us because he guards another opening to your world. The journey is dangerous, but the rewards are great once the trek is over. He's never let us down."

Mr. Iber then asked her, "Have you decided? Are you going to go to Zarlock if the trip is necessary? That's a very long journey."

With resignation, Dwinda said, "I guess Breem and I are elected.

Julie came to me because we've made the trip before and know the way."

"You can count me in," Breem said enthusiastically. Then turning to Cam, he asked, "What about you? It looks like we'll have to get you back to your own world first."

Cam felt as deflated as a tire with a fast leak. He had caught the spirit of adventure and wanted to join them on their trek. Forgetting his wish to return in time to see his father, Cam said, "No! I'm coming too!"

"Are you sure?" Breem asked. "I don't want anything to happen to you while you're visiting."

Cam was determined. "Hold it!" he said, throwing up his hand like a traffic cop. "I won't let you shrink me, so then I won't fit through the opening." He paused. "Anyway, maybe this is why I have the Madra Stone."

"You have a Madra Stone!" Dwinda cried in astonishment. "In that case, you're coming!"

"I guess it's decided," Mr. Iber said. "The three of you, be careful. We don't want anything bad to happen to you."

"We'll do our best," Dwinda said. "We have to get going before it's too late. Come on," she gestured to Cam and Breem, "let's go."

They left the school with calls of "good-bye" and "please be careful," ringing in their ears.

As the trio rushed through the woods to Dwinda's house for provisions, Breem told Cam a little about his friendship with Dwinda.

"Dwinda and I have been best friends most of our lives," he said to Cam as though Dwinda was not there. "At times, I think our friendship makes no sense. She's serious, quiet, and efficient. Her greatest joy is spending time in nature and studying ecology."

A cartoon fly buzzed around Cam's nose, and he waved it away.

"Still, it's exactly Dwinda's practical nature that's kept us together. She helps keep me from getting into things I can't get out of. Dwinda has saved me from making choices that could have led to serious trouble."

Dwinda smiled as Breem spoke. "And I enjoy Breem's zest for life," she said. "My life would be very boring without him. As a matter of fact, it was Breem's sense of adventure that pushed us to see Zarlock the last time. He just wanted to see what it would be like to go there. Now it looks like that trek is working to our advantage."

Eventually, they arrived at Dwinda's house, a small, round cottage nestled at the forest's edge and facing a sunny field. Its thatched, rounded roof was covered with flowering vines. Large, shuttered windows let in plenty of light. Before they even reached the front yard, Cam felt its inviting warmth.

Breem rushed into the house behind Dwinda and motioned for Cam to follow. They got busy packing food and other provisions for the trip. Because they worked together, it didn't take long, and they were ready to leave. They gathered enough supplies to last until they reached Zarlock, in case they went that far. Cam and Breem put packs of food and water on their backs while Dwinda strapped rolls of blankets on hers and they set off on their trip.

Chapter 10

The Desert

After a long and exhausting walk, the trio arrived at the fringes of a bizarre, desert-like area. It was stranger than any pictures of deserts Cam had ever seen. Instead of sand, this ground was covered with tiny, low-growing vines.

"I've never seen a desert with vines all over the ground," he said.

"Stumble-vines are only found in this desert," Dwinda said.

"Stumble-vines?"

"That's what we call them," she said. "Be careful when you walk—it takes practice to get around on the vines because it's so easy to stumble and fall."

Aside from the ground, the desert looked much like the ones he was familiar with. Here and there, short stubby trees and bushes grew in clumps. As with most deserts, this one, too, roasted in the hot sun.

Cam struggled with fatigue. He didn't want to delay his companions. Still, he didn't blame himself for his exhaustion since he'd been going steadily since early morning. His weary body was relieved when Dwinda said, “We’d better stop for the night. It will take hours to get to the Moving Forest, and it looks like the sun will be going down soon.”

It didn’t take the group long to find a comfortable place to settle by a clump of short shrubs. Soon mats were rolled out and covered with warm blankets. They settled comfortably on the twisty vines.

“I brought dried fruits, cheese, bread, and water,” Dwinda said as she opened some small containers and placed them on the ground for all to reach. “I thought we should have something quick and easy and won’t leave a mess.”

After eating, Cam could feel his energy coming back. He chipped in as each one cleaned up behind them. Then Cam had a great idea. “I know what we could do! At home, whenever we camp out for the night, we build a bonfire. Then we sit around the fire, tell scary stories, and sing funny songs. Wanna do that?”

“Yeah! That sounds like fun—let’s do it.” Breem said.

Practical Dwinda had other thoughts. “It does sound like fun; too bad we’re in a desert. The only water we have to put out a fire is our drinking water, and the vines on the ground would catch fire in seconds. It could spread everywhere before we had a chance to put it out.” She turned to Cam, “Do you think we could do it another time, somewhere where it would be safer?”

Though disappointed, Cam knew Dwinda was right. It would be best if they waited for the right time and place for the bonfire. “I didn’t think of that,” he said, his cheeks and ears burning. “I just wanted a bit of excitement.”

“Don’t worry, Cam,” Dwinda said between yawns, “There’ll be plenty of excitement if we go on to Zarlock.”

As the threes settled into their sleeping bags for the night, the darkening sky provided a hush to their world. The crisp shadows, produced by the setting sun, faded into fuzzy, gray, indistinct forms. Unnoticed by the travelers, one of these shadowy forms moved. A low, raspy voice whispered, “So you want adventure, do you? Then an adventure you shall have! But it will not involve going to see Zarlock. You will never make it!” The harsh voice continued as the mysterious shadow faded into the dark. “Welcome to Worpple, Cam.”

Chapter 11

The Gigglewits

As the early morning sun prepared to fix its balmy gaze upon the world, Cam, Breem, and Dwinda were sprawled on the ground deep in sleep. A soft giggling sound in the distance enticed Cam toward wakefulness. Gradually, the nearing parade of music came closer and closer. It was louder and louder—until the air filled with a giggling-gurgling racket.

Rubbing his eyes as he sat up, Cam was disoriented. The continuous noisy chuckle sounded like a gang of children laughing in glee. The noise brought Cam back to reality and the strange desert. He was surrounded by peculiar orange animals that looked like a cross between a snail and a turtle—sort of. About five inches tall and eight inches long, their heads were topped with two antennae that ended in balled eyes. Their lizard-like eyes moved independently and gazed in different directions at the same time.

As the little creatures headed directly toward Cam, he became nervous and wondered if they were dangerous. "Hey, what's happening?" He turned toward his companions, who had also been awakened by the noise. "What do they want? How come they're not bothering you? Will they hurt me?" His concern flowed into the air like streamers at a party. Breem and Dwinda's broad smiles reassured him, and he relaxed a bit.

Sitting yoga-style, Breem propped his head in his hands and explained, "Gigglewits are harmless. They definitely won't go away until they're ready, so you might as well relax and enjoy yourself."

Kneeling, Dwinda busied herself, making sure the food was protected from the Gigglewits' enormous appetites. "I think they want to play with you. Just go along with them, and they'll get bored after a while and leave."

Cam unwrapped the blanket he was tangled in and wondered aloud what to do next. "How am I supposed to play with them? Like with a dog or cat at home?"

His question was answered before the others could say a word. One Gigglewit grabbed the lace of his runner lying at the foot of his makeshift bed. Before he could react, six of them had the laces of both shoes in their mouths as they ran away at breathless speed.

"Hey! Those are my runners. I need them," he shouted after the funny creatures. Jumping up, he started after them and tripped on the stumble-vines. Within seconds, five of the strange little creatures had climbed on top of him. Their little feet tickled his sides as they crawled on his body.

"Okay, you guys, it's not polite to climb on the company." He laughed.

As he carefully plucked the orange creatures from his body, he looked over and noticed the ones with his shoes had stopped. To Cam, it seemed they were watching to see if he was coming.

"Those bugs are checking me out," he called to his companions. Breem and Dwinda were engrossed in the antics going on in front of them.

He wanted to get up and go after his footwear, but he no sooner took off two creatures when three more climbed onboard. They tickled him, and, before long, he laughed loudly as he rolled on the ground.

"Hey! Cut that out! Oh, no, help! They're tickling me. Help, oh no. I'm too ticklish, heelllp!"

A short distance away, the ground-vines stirred as if someone were walking on them. Yet, there was no one to be seen. A sinister snicker might have been heard if Cam was not making so much noise.

"So, you want adventure, my young friend," the menacing voice scoffed. "Here is a small taste of what is to come."

Without warning, one of the Gigglewits reached out and bit Cam hard on the finger. He jumped up, shrieking with pain as he shook his hand. Snapping creatures fell like rocks to the ground.

Shocked and annoyed, he yelled. "Hey! I thought you said these things were harmless. One of them just bit me!"

Breem and Dwinda rushed to him. Blood seeped through from his finger and left splatters on the ground.

Abruptly, a loud, shrill cry pierced the air from behind. The group twirled around. The travelers were stunned to find two Gigglewits tearing at each other.

"Quick—get back!" Breem cried.

As the astonished group watched, three more animals began fighting. Before long, fights were in progress all around the travelers, and several of the beautiful creatures lay dead on the ground.

Cam had a hard time understanding what just happened, and he scanned the faces of Breem and Dwinda to give him a clue. Would they be able to explain this disturbing turn of events? He was disappointed to realize they were as confused as he was. His friends also watched with their mouths agape.

The fighting soon stopped, and the surviving Gigglewits wandered away from the group, snarling and snapping as they left. Then, as quickly as it had started, the quarreling ceased, and the orange creatures calmly wandered off, leaving behind a chilly silence and the bodies of their companions littering the area.

Dwinda wrapped Cam's finger with a strip of cloth torn from a sheet of bedding. In a frightened voice, Breem commented, "I've never seen Gigglewits act like that before. Have you, Dwinda?"

"No, never," she said sadly. "I wonder if this is what Julie was talking about."

Just then, a bird sitting on one of the shrubs shot up with a loud screech and flew off into the sky as a menacing laugh filled the air. In unison, the group spun toward the sound but saw nothing.

The hair on Cam's neck stood erect. "What's going on?" he

bawled. "Where's that laughter coming from?"

"I don't know," Dwinda said in alarm, "but I can feel the evil in the air."

"So can I," Breem said in a quiet and gloomy voice.

"Creepy. I've got goose flesh," Cam said. "What do we do now?" Once more, his companions' faces told him they were as mystified and distressed as Cam.

The malicious laughter stopped, and the tense silence that followed was cut through by a voice that sounded like a pit of snakes talking. "Be prepared, my young friends. We will meet again."

Suddenly, the air brightened as if a light had been switched on, and the sinister, invisible presence was gone.

"Wh—what was that all about?" Breem stammered.

"I've never heard anything like it," Dwinda said, "and I hope it never comes back."

As the stunned friends stared vacantly, the air around them once more began to shimmer. Jumping back, Cam poised to fight, his fists raised for action, adrenalin coursing through his body, ready for whatever appeared. As Julie's holographic form was seen suspended in the air before them, he sighed with relief and lowered his hands.

"You have just encountered the cause of the Gigglewits' strange behavior," Julie explained within each traveler's mind. "The voice you just heard came from the evil force which has entered our world."

Alarmed, both Breem and Dwinda spoke together as they pleaded with Julie for directions.

"What can we do?" Breem gasped.

"It felt so horrid," Dwinda said. She shuddered, "I don't know if we're strong enough to battle it."

"It's clear now that you must travel to Zarlock," Julie said. "I'll watch over you for as long as my powers allow, then you'll be on your own."

As she finished her message, Julie's form faded like butter on hot toast.

Cam stood transfixed. He could still feel the adrenalin pumping through him, but now there was no enemy and nowhere to unload his tension. As Cam looked at his friends, he tried to guess their ability to deal with the evil force that had invaded their land. Dwinda didn't seem like a fighter, and he doubted Breem had any fighting skills.

Staring at them, he made his judgment at that moment; he decided he was the only one who could save Worpple—that is, if it was going to be saved at all.

"We have a very long journey ahead of us," Dwinda's voice broke the silence. "We'd better eat and get out of here right away."

While the group prepared for their journey, Cam remembered his shoes and went looking for them. His search, however, was in vain.

"Did either of you see which way those orange turtle-things went with my shoes?" he asked.

"Your shoes?" said Dwinda, "I'd forgotten all about them."

"We'll help you look," Breem said.

The next half hour was spent searching, but no shoes were to be seen anywhere. Cam gave up—his shoes had vanished.

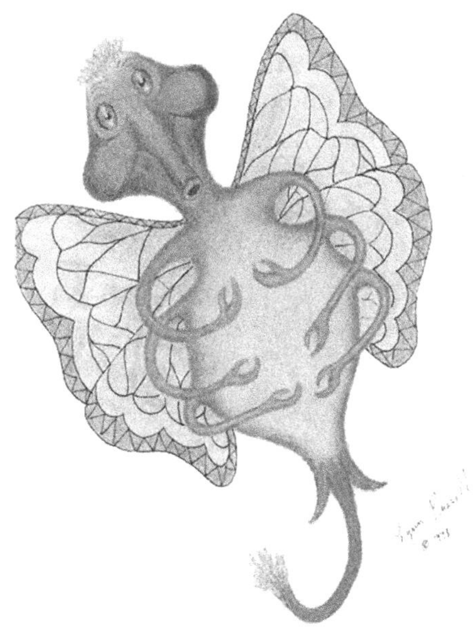

Chapter 12

Marvel

Hours later, Cam limped across the desert on feet of raging, angry pain. He had become so dependent on shoes that he hadn't considered what it would be like without them. Walking over hard-packed ground covered by the tangled vines had become unbearable. Now, with each step, a throbbing agony shot through his feet, up his back, and into his head. His stomach joined in, and he felt like he was going to throw up at any moment.

When walking became too painful, Breem and Dwinda offered their shoulders for him to lean on. This helped a bit as Cam could take some of the pressure off his screaming feet. Then, at least, the vines didn't dig into his feet as much. Still, he knew if he didn't get shoes on soon, he wouldn't be able to complete the journey. *How would Worpple be saved then*?

These thoughts gnawed at him like a mouse creating a new hole until he looked up. What was that jutting out from the tangled vines? At first, he had a hard time seeing it because it just looked like a large purple smudge in the distance. It did not take long before he realized it was an even, purple, grassy area. Cam was filled with great relief and joy. He could almost feel its silky coolness on his feet from where he stood.

"I never knew I could be this happy at the sight of grass." He laughed. Letting go of their shoulders, he slumped to his hands and knees. As though he were in a movie on fast forward, he crawled to the welcome sight. The instant he felt the grass beneath him, he spread out on his back like a sunbather on soft sand. It felt like he was lying on a smooth, cooling blanket of velvet. The three laughed as he waved his painful feet in the air. "Ah," he groaned in ecstasy, "I'm in heaven, and I didn't even have to die."

The gentle breeze stirred, and the air felt soothing as though someone was softly blowing on his burning feet. Relief surged through him, washing away the pain like a comforting medication.

Breem and Dwinda joined him on the grass and soaked in the pleasure of the moment. "It seems to me this is a perfect time to eat," Dwinda said.

"Don't let me stop you." Cam laughed as he grabbed hungrily for the food bags.

Half an hour later, with a full stomach and a chance to rest, Cam felt able to travel again. Even though his feet were still tender, it didn't come close to the pain he experienced walking on the vines. His stomach and back had settled down, and he felt more optimistic about completing the journey. Lying on his side on the fresh velvet grass with his head propped on his hand, he gazed in the direction they were preparing to travel. Off in the distance, he could see a vast forest.

Dwinda's eyes followed the same direction and said, "Don't enter the Moving Forest, Cam. It's a dangerous place."

"That's for sure," Breem said. "You could get killed doing something like that."

Staring at the forest in the distance, Cam wondered how it was dangerous. Just as he was about to ask, he noticed a gigantic butterfly circling overhead. His thoughts about the forest vanished as he stared at this new magnificent creature.

Just then, the butterfly spotted the travelers and swooped down toward them. It landed by them with wonder on its happy face.

Cam had never seen a friendly butterfly before and especially one this size. He leaned toward the gracious creature for a closer look.

The butterfly had a round, iridescent-blue body that ended in a long tail of the same color. Cam wondered if his eyes were deceiving him because this creature was the size of an eagle. Its wings were pink with glitters of gold. They seemed so delicate he could almost see through them. The butterfly's head was diamond-shaped, with the top coming to a rounded point that held a tuft of blue hair. Its fat, round cheeks ended in a long tubular nose that almost looked like a horn. Its golden eyes gleamed bright and shiny and appeared very friendly.

Excited, Cam cried out, "Beautiful! What is it?"

"That's a whooper." Dwinda said. "Whoopers are actually very rare. There are only a few in the world at any one time. They get their names from the noise they make with their noses."

As if to demonstrate, the whooper suddenly released a loud and prolonged "WHOOOP!"

Staring with his jaw dropped open, Cam could not believe his ears—this creature sounded exactly like Marcy when she laughed. "This can't be real! This must be some kind of joke. I have a friend back in my world that sometimes gets called 'Whooper' 'cause of the way she laughs. This creature sounds just like her!" Turning again to the strange butterfly, he asked, "Is it friendly—it looks intelligent, can it understand me?"

"Sure," Dwinda answered, "whoopers are very friendly. They're much like your dolphins—they can understand quite a lot but can't communicate in our language. This one's a female—the females are blue, and males are green."

Bending down to stroke the whooper's head, he spoke softly to her. "Hey there, girl, you're really beautiful, you know. Whooper is a terrible name for you. I think I'll call you, ah—Marvel!"

Marvel responded by rolling over in mid-air and exposed her tummy for him to rub. It didn't take him long to discover that Marvel's wings weren't quite as delicate as they appeared. She proved to be a hearty, roughhousing companion as they played together on the grass, rolling, laughing, and whooping up a noisy commotion. He remembered playing with his grandparent's dog like this. Sadly, his family wasn't allowed to have pets in the projects. He missed the joy and pleasure of just rolling around with an animal and being a kid again. When the small group continued their journey, they now counted four, with Marvel following closely by Cam.

Chapter 13

The Moving Forest

As the travelers drew close to the Moving Forest, Cam noticed something on the ground to his right. It was near the forest's edge, and his curiosity drove him to cautiously limp over to the object.

Astonished, he stared in disbelief at the scene before him. A twisted, strange beast lay dead on the ground. The creature almost resembled a brown dog with coarse, shaggy hair. It was about the size of a beagle hound, but that was where any similarity to an Earth creature ended. An evil snarl was plastered on its ugly face, and a long, pointed horn grew from the center of its head. Clearly, this beast had been fighting. It was covered with blood and gashes from an attacker's teeth. Worst of all, the smell coming from the creature almost took away Cam's breath. It was like putrid garbage mixed with rotten eggs. Yet none of that captured Cam's attention—no. It was his shoes lying just beyond the animal's head that fascinated him.

"Hey guys, come and look at this!" he coughed in amazement as he held his nose with one hand and stretched out his other hand to grab his shoes.

Suddenly, from above, came a loud "whoop." Faster than he would have thought possible, Marvel swooped in front of him just as the dog-like beast leaped for his throat. Marvel's actions caused Cam to jump back just in time for the bared fangs of the vile creature to catch on the neck of his T-shirt and make a small rip. Then, with neither sense nor reason, the repulsive freak flopped back down dead, as if nothing had happened.

Terror rushed through Cam as he felt adrenalin race through his body, ready for action. Fear crashed through his senses. He looked around, trying to make some sense of what had just happened. He stared at the dead animal and tried to judge the craziness in this mysterious land. How could the dead thing lying on the ground almost tear out his throat?

It couldn't have happened. That was all there was to it. It was just his imagination. Cam knew it could never have happened because there the creature was, lying completely still in the grip of death. A puff of wind stirred the brute's fur and provided the only movement of the detestable beast.

What type of place had he come to? Was it all just his mind playing tricks on him? As he struggled to make sense from the senseless, Dwinda rushed over and confirmed for him that what had happened was real.

"Oh no!" she cried as she reached out to him. "Are you all right?"

A rush of anger raced through him. This place was just too weird. He tensed for attack and yelled, "What is this place? Evil voices from nowhere, disappearing shoes, and dead creatures that attack. What have I gotten myself into?" he asked as Dwinda stared at him with a look of concern.

"I don't blame you for being upset," Breem said as soon he was able to catch up to his companions. "I've never seen anything like that before. What's going on?"

Cam felt self-conscious about lashing out in anger and tried to cover himself. Calmly he said, "Sorry, Dwinda, I'm okay…just scared; that's all. I wouldn't be if Marvel hadn't warned me, though." Hugging the whooper around her neck and patting her head, he said, "If she hadn't jumped in when she did, I'd be finished! I was positive that hideous thing was dead." Pausing, he pointed toward the beast on the ground. "Look, it has my shoes!"

Once again, his attention was focused on how he could get his shoes. The sun came out from behind a cloud and highlighted his runners like a solo act on stage. His feet were so sensitive he could hardly think, other than getting something on them.

Cam moved to the edge of the forest and stared into it. With his hands on his hips, he thought, *If I got a branch from one of these trees, I'd be able to pull my shoes far enough away from that dog-thing to pick them up.*

As he stood deep in thought, Breem and Dwinda said, "Cam, move away from the forest." Their repeated cautions only frustrated him. *Why were those guys warning me? I can't see anything moving; in fact, all I see is peace and tranquility. There's even a path running right through the forest that goes where we want to go.* The sunlight danced through the trees and sprinkled an invitation.

Dwinda moved up beside him. "Cam, please listen. We can't go that way. We have to go around the forest."

"I'm not leaving 'til I get my shoes," he said. "I don't see why you guys insist we go around the forest…it looks okay to me. I can see right into it. I can make it—watch!"

Just as he was about to boldly plunge into the forest, Marvel swooped down and blocked the entrance.

"Marvel, get outta the way," he said loudly. "I just wanna get a branch or stick from one of these trees so I can get my shoes away from that beast."

Marvel flew up in the air. He didn't see where she was going because, in his mind, she was agreeing with his actions.

Breem and Dwinda yelled to stop Cam while he pushed himself into the forest. His shoes were by that dangerous beast, and he was determined to get them. He didn't feel the vine that quickly slithered around his leg with the silence of a snake. Within seconds, he was engulfed by dozens of branches and vines as they grabbed at him and yanked him into the air. One leg and arm were entangled in the branches, leaving him dangling sideways off the ground at an awkward angle. His free arm and leg splayed out in an ungainly illustration of someone halfway through a cartwheel. Terror ripped through him. "Help—I can't get out! Help me!"

Chapter 14

Stuck

"Oh, Cam! what have you done?" Dwinda cried out. "We warned you!" With her head down and her hands clasped behind her, she stomped across the front of the forest. After going a few paces, she spun around and tramped back the other direction, with no apparent purpose to her pacing. Finally, she turned to Breem. "What are we going to do? We've got to do something...but what?"

Breem was busy wringing his hands and frozen to where he stood as he stared at Cam. "I…I don't know what to do either. If we go in after him, we'll be hanging too. I've never heard of anyone getting out and telling how they did it. Why didn't he just listen?"

Overhead, Marvel looped through the air in dizzying swirls and squawked her loud whoops. In the forest, Cam continued to holler for help.

While everyone was busy giving up hope, the air began to shimmer in the afternoon sun. Relieved, Dwinda gasped, "Oh, thank goodness, Julie's here to help."

Marvel too became more settled as she flew down to witness

Julie's arrival. The shimmer materialized into Julie's holographic form directly in front of the dangling boy.

Cam continued to struggle. The more he strained, the tighter the plants gripped his body. Panic sent acid from his stomach into his mouth. He was being squeezed to death.

"Cam," Julie said, "stop struggling, or you'll die. If you want to live, then you must listen to me."

This urgent appeal came directly into Cam's mind, and he finally noticed Julie before him. Gradually her soft voice had a calming effect until he could listen and realize that she was his only hope for survival.

"If you lash against the branches holding you, they'll continue to tighten their grip more and more," Julie said. "So, calm down and keep still and quiet."

Cam felt himself giving in to Julie's commands. Later, he could never describe what happened to soothe him so quickly. Was it because Julie's message had gone directly into his head? Was it her soft voice that sent him into a trance? Whatever it was, the reaction was almost immediate. In exchange for his sudden calm, the branches stopped their incessant tightening around his body.

"Remember, you're a stranger here in Worpple," Julie said. "There are some things you don't understand."

Off in the distance, as though in a fog, Cam could see Breem, Dwinda, and Marvel watching from beyond the forest's edge. They were like phantoms that didn't entirely penetrate his awareness. His complete concentration was centered on what was happening between him and Julie. As he watched her form, he was surprised by the gentleness and warmth he felt radiating from her. He would have been less surprised had she been angry and scolded him.

"Cam, you have a special light within you that you do not yet know about. With the help of the Madra Stone, you will learn of the special ability you possess and how to use it."

"I don't understand." Cam grunted from his position in the entangled branches.

"You'll understand in time, but right now, let's get you out of this mess. I have some things to teach you."

Cam wasn't sure about a cartoon flower woman teaching him stuff, and he thought her timing sucked. Now, while he's being crushed by trees, she wants to show him something. Then again, when he considered the alternative—strangulation by these vines, for example—he was more willing to listen.

Julie's voice filled his head, "You need your first lesson about Rainbow Power.'"

"Rainbow Power?"

"Animals, fish, birds, and even plants share a special element with you," Julie said, "they all have a life force. This life force is your connection with them. It is the essence of you and each creature in Worpple and in your world too. It's what gives each existence its own special spark. This connection, blended with the special light and caring, is what we call Rainbow Power."

Cam remembered hearing about some kind of connection to other life forms, but he never paid attention. Now he wished he had.

Julie continued, "Even though we can't see Rainbow Power, it's still an essential part of our union with all of life. Just as the colors in a rainbow are united to white light in a prism. To get out of the Moving Forest, you need to understand and use the Rainbow Power I'm telling you about. Once you really understand the connectedness of all life, then you'll find that you're able to appeal to the plants that hold you."

"What?" a confused Cam asked. "Are you saying these plants can talk to me?"

A mild breeze splashed through the trees and sent their leaves into a shiver of movement as though in answer to Cam's question. He remained in his partial cartwheel pose and concentrated on Julie's words.

"When you understand Rainbow Power, the idea of communicating with them will be less confusing."

Julie's voice was clear and firm in Cam's mind, and he wondered how he had ever doubted learning from her a moment ago.

"Now," she said, "concentrate on these plants and how your shared life force connects you to them."

"Okay, so, once I'm connected to them, what do I say?"

"Why," Julie hesitated as if she was shocked at the question. "Share with them that you know and understand this special bond with them."

Cam cringed at the suggestion. How, at a time like this, was he supposed to feel a special bond with these things? "Too weird," Cam said. "Julie, these branches are trying to kill me. How am I supposed to feel a special bond with them?"

"Come on, Cam. You've got to try." Breem's sense of urgency rang through his words.

Standing at the edge of the forest, Dwinda called to him. "Cam, you don't have a choice—others in your situation are usually killed."

Although Cam still hung off the ground, he was more frightened than hurt, and Dwinda's warning didn't ease his fear. "Okay, okay. I'll give it a try, even though I'm confused."

Cam turned to Julie. "Where do I start?"

"Let's start with you," Julie said. "There's a part of you deep down inside that's the real you. This element is the same no matter where you are, no matter whom you're with, and it never grows old."

Julie's soft sing-song voice had a hypnotic effect on Cam. He began to feel the smooth floating feeling he felt when he was in bed falling asleep.

Julie continued talking to him, "That special part feels the same now as when you were two, or five, or eight. It's the piece of you that knows when you're doing something you shouldn't. And it also knows what's true and what's a lie. It's very wise."

Caught in the trance of Julie's voice, Cam lowered his head and closed his eyes to concentrate. He remembered a time when he was a small child. He watched a ladybug in the backyard, and he recalled being fascinated by this tiny creature's bravery. Why didn't it fly away from him the way other winged creatures did?

As he remembered this, Cam became aware of a side of himself that was unchanged from that moment in early childhood. Cam had never paid attention to that part of himself before that was unaffected by age—he just knew it was very wise if only he would listen to it.

Now Cam thought he understood what Julie was talking about. He raised his head to her, "Now what?" he asked just as he heard a small creature scurry through the underbrush.

"Turn your attention to the branches and vines holding you. That deep, wise center of yourself will help you feel your common bond with them."

Listening to Julie's instructions, a thought flashed into his head that seemed to come from nowhere. Think positive thoughts, he heard from deep in his mind, think about love. Ah, that idea must be coming from that wise place Julie spoke about.

Cam concentrated—what did he really enjoy? Football sprang to his mind. But how was thinking about football going to help him get out of this mess? Still, happiness flooded him when he thought of his favorite pastime. He remembered Marcy and saw her laughing and squealing as she sprayed water at him. This thought brought feelings of greater happiness and joy. He thought of his mom, dad, and little sister and the fun times they had together at family picnics, and he allowed his love for them to fill his heart.

Cam opened his eyes and looked at the branches that held his body in their grip. The realization they also shared this same living force overwhelmed him. They were just like him, just like him. Imagine!

Slowly, so slow that he wasn't sure if it were his imagination working overtime, Cam began to feel the shackles loosening their grip. At that moment, a surge of pure joy for the plants and the life they both shared rushed through him. They were letting him go. He was saved. His body lowered to the ground, and he raced out of the Moving Forest to safety and freedom and fell to the ground.

Julie's form remained in the air watching to be sure that Cam was completely safe and unhurt.

"How did that work, Julie?" Cam asked as he sat on the ground.

"The plants and vines only want to capture outsiders for food. When you connected with them, it seemed to them that they had captured a part of themselves, and they had to let go."

Now that Cam was free and unhurt, Julie's form faded from view as if being blown away by a puff of wind. Before long, all that was left of her was her gentle voice saying, "Goodbye and good luck."

Breem raced over to his friend, closely followed by Dwinda and Marvel. "Are you all right? Can you get up?" he asked as he reached out to help Cam.

With Breem's help, Cam struggled to his feet, shaken but not hurt. "Was that scary or what?" he asked. The realization he'd just faced death twice in the last ten minutes broke through his relief, and a strange feeling tingled through him. He felt filled with a new energy that he'd never known before. His fresh understanding of life made him feel more invigorated and alive. Life seemed to have taken on a happier meaning.

Chapter 15

The Evil Magician

"**W**hoop," Cam heard Marvel cry close by him. She sounded relieved that Cam was saved. Cam groaned when he heard her mournful sound. "Oh man, I'm sorry, Marvel. Are you okay?" A sound almost like a purr escaped her as Cam threw his arms around the whooper.

"I love fun and adventure, Cam, but this is not what I had in mind," Breem said in a voice mixed with annoyance and relief. "I was so scared—if anything were to happen to you, I'd feel responsible. We have to make sure you get home alive."

With the force of a football thumping his head, Cam realized the fright he had given everyone. Looking at the ground, he apologized. "No, I'm the one who's responsible. You guys told me not to go in and—and I didn't listen." He reflected on what Julie said about him being a stranger here. "I'll work harder at paying attention."

Just then, Cam remembered his shoes. "Oh, no," he said. "I need my shoes. That's what I was trying to do when I went into the forest. Now how am I gonna get them away from that dog-thing?"

With a whoop, Marvel flew over to where the beast lay and picked up Cam's shoes with her feet—the dead animal never moved. She quickly brought the runners back to Cam and laid them on the ground before him like a gift.

"Wow, Marvel, thanks." Cam dropped to the ground and began the struggle of putting shoes on very sore feet.

Without warning, Marvel let out a loud and frightened "Whoooop." Cringing at Cam's side, she snuggled against him, trembling with fear. Before he could ask what was wrong, the air began to shimmer. Could it be Julie—back so soon?

The shimmering gradually became a tall man-like creature cloaked in a long black cape that almost reached the ground. The breeze fluttered the cape and revealed high black boots. He looked like a giant snake wrapped in a cloak. His yellow eyes had pupils with slits that ran sideways across his iris. His long snake-like nose and mouth gave Cam shivers when he licked nonexistent lips with a forked tongue that slithered from his mouth displaying threatening fangs. They looked like they could easily puncture his skin and deliver the creature's poisonous venom. His green hands matched the color of his face and ended in long claw-like nails.

Cam crammed on his remaining shoe and sprang to his feet, leaving the laces to dangle. "Now what's happening?" he bellowed in frustration. It seemed to him this journey was one disaster after another. "Who're you?" When he stared at the ugly creature's eyes, he felt an uneasy knot twist in his stomach. One look at this thing, and Cam knew they were in grave danger.

The vile brute threw his head back, laughing gleefully. It was the same sinister laughter the threesome had heard in the desert earlier. Arrogantly, he circled the astonished travelers. "I am the Magician," the monster said in the same hissing voice from the desert. "I am the one you search for. I am known as the Evil Magician, and I am the one who can make dead animals attack. I will bring this world to its knees."

Cam thought of some of the bullies from his world, but they didn't come close to this guy. The only place he could remember seeing beasts as sinister as this one was in his computer games. But this guy was real. If Cam were honest, not even Jason presented such a fiendish picture as this creature. He rushed in front of the others, wanting to protect them. "You don't scare me; I've met tyrants like you before."

"Ah, yes. Cam. Our little visitor from the Earth dimension," the Magician said, "I know all about you. Tell me, Cam, can the tough friends from your world do this?" The Evil Magician pointed his finger at the dead animal.

At once, the dead dog-thing lying in a heap leaped up from the ground. Turning its bloodied head their way, the monster's vacant eyes began to glow red, life-like. With a jerk and snarl, it lunged its battered body toward them.

Everyone scattered. With a tremendous shriek, Marvel took flight. Cam and Dwinda fled toward the desert, followed by Breem.

Poor Breem's legs were just too short to put a safe distance between him and the ghastly beast. Breem fell to the ground with an incoherent scream, and seconds later, the dog was on top of him.

Hearing Breem's cry, Cam whirled around and raced back to help his friend. He summoned up the strength of a quarterback and gave the dog a vicious kick. It flew through the air and landed on its back, yards away from Breem. The brute once more struggled to its feet and pounced at Cam. Cam fled as though he were running the football to a touchdown. Without pausing, he raced right past the watching Magician toward the Moving Forest.

Cam stopped abruptly at the forest's edge, remembering all too well what had happened in the woods just moments before. Thinking quickly, he whirled around to face his attacker. Just as the dog leaped toward him, Cam threw himself sideways to the ground. The momentum of the creature's lunge sent it hurling into the forest. Seconds later, the ugly beast was entangled in the Moving Forest branches and vines, just as Cam had hoped.

The other travelers watched from behind the shelter of low shrubs.

"Ah, I see you are a worthy opponent, Cam," the Magician said as he rubbed his dry, raspy hands together in glee. "I shall enjoy my encounters with your world. After I have ravaged this sickly hovel of love, I will pay a visit there."

"How'd you know about my world?" Cam asked.

"I know a lot more than you realize. Once I have ripped this world apart, I'll gain complete power. I will enter your world through the tiny openings being protected by those love-mongers, Julie and Zarlock. Then everyone in your world will become my slaves just as everyone here will. Those who don't obey me will be tortured until they are ready to follow my commands or die."

Jason and his gang came to Cam's mind. Except now, the stakes were much higher. Now he was responsible for saving both this world and his own Earth.

"What are you talking about, man," Cam shouted, "go right now. The Earth would turn you into blubbering mush if you ever did manage to make it there. You ugly freak."

"What an amusing boy you are." The Magician leered. "It is clear you do not know my powers; otherwise, you would be sniveling at my feet just like your friends over there. I will go to your world when I'm ready. And I am not ready yet. I am not finished here. I must defeat the contaminating love-disciples that guard the entrances to your world. That will be the greatest joy of all." The Magician threw back his head, releasing a bloodcurdling laugh. As his form vanished in the air, he left behind only his laughter's ominous echo.

Once the Magician was gone, the others joined Cam and gathered their belongings. With one last glance at the dog creature stuck in the trees, together, they began their journey around the edge of the forest.

Chapter 16

Wixer's Shack

As daylight dwindled to a swirling murky soup of deep purple and gray, the foursome came upon a tumbled-down shack hidden in the woods. Cam was glad he had the others with him, or he would never have made it alone. He couldn't tell when they had left the dangerous Moving Forest and entered a thickly wooded area that looked almost the same. Deep in these safe woods, they found the shack with a flickering light at its windows.

After an eventful day, there had been little talk as Cam and the others were lost in their own feelings. As the light of the day began to dwindle, exhaustion overtook each of them. Cam wondered where they would spend the night. The sight of the shack tucked back into the trees helped everyone's spirits rise. Perhaps here they would find refreshments and a place to spend the night.

Dwinda sighed as she flopped down in the middle of the path and rested on the blanket roll. "Oh good, my feet are killing me. I don't think I could have walked another step, even if we hadn't found this place."

Breem plopped himself down beside Dwinda and shared the blanket roll. "Oh, yes! Five minutes with my feet up—just five minutes." He moaned, propping them up on his backpack. Even Marvel found a comfortable perch on a nearby branch, wrapped herself in her wings, and rested quietly.

Cam was also tired, but his caution was more powerful than his desire to rest. Although they'd left the Moving Forest behind, every movement made him jump and sent shivers of dread through him. Now, ominous shadows of night deepened, and, in his mind, they would soon reveal a terrifying black void. After too many close calls on this trip, Cam had begun to imagine threatening dread waiting for him behind every tree. They simply had to find a safe place to stay for the night. He didn't think he could manage a whole night of fear.

Cam crept to the door of the shack. He wasn't getting a good feeling. The nerves in the back of his neck felt creepy. "Hey," he called, "Is anybody home?"

It was a wonder they even found the shack at all. It was set back in the forest behind several trees. Its drab walls were covered with vines and branches. In the gloom, it seemed almost buried in the trees. It was Marvel who had brought the place to their attention.

Just as Cam lifted his arm to knock, out of the corner of his eye he saw something move. In an instant, a large bird swooped down from a nearby tree. The bird barely missed Cam's head as it pounced on what looked like a snake slithering around the side of the house. Revulsion filled Cam as he watched the bird fly off with the snake clutched in its claws. He wasn't sure this place was such a good idea after all. On second thought, this was the sort of place where he expected the Magician to live.

"You guys sure you wanna stay here?"

The two lumps on the ground, leaning against the blanket roll, emphatically replied in unison, "Yes."

"What about you, Marvel? You seem to be good at sensing danger. Do you think it's a good idea to stay here?"

Without answering, Marvel snuggled deeper into her wings and tried to sleep.

"I guess if it's okay with all of you, then I must be just getting the jitters."

Once again, Cam turned toward the door and prepared to knock. A mean-looking giant filled the doorway and glared down at him. "What do you want?" The massive beast's voice sounded like the deep rumbling of a huge truck.

Cam felt intimidated and alone. He held up his palms to the creature and backed away from the door. "Ah…noth... nothing; nope, not a thing." He had discovered that even though everything in this dimension was in cartoon form, he could be hurt just easily as in his own stable world.

The giant, light brown monster in the doorway stood at least a head taller than Cam and Breem. His massive size and mighty shoulders looked powerful. His long, thin, tan-colored face was surrounded by a large mane that encircled his head and made it look bigger than it was. The creature's long antenna at the top of his head wiggled when he talked as if he was searching for hidden information that Cam could not imagine. Yet, his most outstanding features were his enormous black eyes that missed little.

Although the monster was snarling, his manner seemed to ease a little. "Nobody ever comes to see me unless they want something, so you must want something too."

This guy is no worse than the Magician. Cam plucked up his courage. *I was willing to face him so I can do this now.* He ran his fingers through his hair, leaving a red nest of bushy tresses for his effort.

He took a step toward the creature, stating a bit too forcefully, "Congratulations, man, you win the prize. We do want something."

In a flash, gloomy sadness dominated the creature's huge eyes. Cam watched, astonished as a tear quietly slid down the creature's furry cheek. As he sighed heavily, his massive shoulders and arms sagged toward the ground. The rapid alteration in the beast's expression was not what Cam had expected.

"I thought so," the beast's deep voice whispered. "Well, the answer is no, so go away."

Cam realized that something was really bothering this large creature for him to change so much from one moment to the next. His thoughts turned to the needs of his small party, and he was not about to be turned away quite that easily. They had traveled a long way and were tired; the night was coming, and this was the only house they had seen since they left Dwinda's. Beyond the door, he could see only darkness and the shadows of a fire dancing on the walls. Strangely, he felt a sense of responsibility to this creature to explain the terrible threat that was sweeping Worpple. "Are you sure?" He asked. "Even if it means saving your life?"

The dejected beast grabbed the door, intending to close it in his face. "It doesn't matter. I don't care."

Cam thought the creature sounded like himself when he was more hurt than angry. Before he was totally shut out, he'd better think of something to say and fast.

"That's strange, 'cause you seem like one of the good guys," he rushed out with the first thing that came to his mind. His first thought was of Jason and his gang. *What would I like to hear from them?* "I bet if we tried, we could probably be friends. I've never met anyone like you before. You're impressive."

The creature's eyes opened wide, and he said, "What—I don't understand."

"You, I'm talking about you. I think you're all right."

"Yeah, well, you're pretty interesting-looking yourself. I've never seen anything like you before, either."

"That's 'cause I am different. I'm from the Earth dimension. I'm here visiting."

As he spoke, another visible change came over the beast at the door. His eyes became lighter, and his shoulders straightened.

"How did you get here from another dimension?"

"My friend over there brought me." He pointed toward Breem. "It sure is interesting."

The being's face softened as he said, "I guess I could listen to what you have to say."

Glad to be making headway, he wasted no time explaining what was happening.

"We're on a very critical mission. We've traveled a long way and want some time to recuperate, a place to rest before we continue." Pausing to catch his breath, Cam added, "Hey! You could come with us. That'd be terrific!"

The creature looked at him in bewilderment. "I don't understand. You want me to join you? Where are you going? Why?"

Cam was thrilled. Maybe they would be able to stay after all. Then this big, muscular guy could join them and help him with the task of saving Worpple. In one great breath, he explained about the Evil Magician and his hideous plans. "After he's destroyed everyone in your world, he's gonna go to my world and destroy it, too," he said.

Astonishment and concern marked the creature's face. "Exactly when and where did this Magician enter Worpple?"

Something about the creature's reaction concerned Cam. Hesitantly he answered, "Sometime yesterday afternoon—near here—why?"

"No! It can't be. This is horrible. I didn't mean to do anything that terrible."

Chapter 17

The Spell

While Cam and the creature were talking, Breem, Dwinda, and Marvel sat back and let Cam handle the situation. With the beast's last words, a jolt of shock lit their faces. Breem and Dwinda flashed up to a sitting position, and Marvel pulled her head out from under her wing. They all stared at the beast in astonishment.

Cam's mouth gaped open. "You…why?" he stammered. Anger flooded him. "What's with you? What did you do?"

The creature's shoulders curved inward as he looked down at the ground shamefully. "I was mad because nobody liked me. I wanted to pay them back. But I didn't want to bring evil into the world and destroy it. My name's Wixer, by the way, and I guess all of you had better come in while I explain."

"This better be good." Cam grumbled as he stepped over the threshold.

As the group, including Marvel, crowded into Wixer's gloomy and sparsely furnished shack, the big guy busied himself with lighting a few candles and making tea. Once everyone was seated at the rickety kitchen table and introductions had been made, Wixer told his story.

"Ever since I was young, the other guys at school bullied and ridiculed me. I was too big and frightened them, or my eyes were too scary, and I moved funny. On and on it went."

"Yeah, I know what that's like," Cam said. "Guys in my world push me around and make fun of me too. I get mad, and sometimes they stop—all except a bully named Jason, that is."

"Well, after a while, I got mad too," Wixer said, "and they stopped, all right. Then they avoided me completely." Wixer stopped talking. His large sad eyes looked down at the ground. "So, one day, I found this place in the woods. Now I live like a hermit. I hardly ever see anyone."

Marvel released a forlorn sounding "Whoop."

"It gets so lonely sometimes I can barely stand it." Wixer continued, encouraged by her understanding. "At least I don't have to put up with their stupid taunting, except sometimes, I feel so alone and angry, I just wanted to pay them back. That's what I was doing when I brought this evil Magician into our world. Trying to see if I could get the other guys to like me."

True to form, practical Dwinda wanted to hear the main point. "So, what happened? How did you do that?" she asked as she sipped her tea.

"Yesterday morning, I was out in the yard digging for food when I moved a big boulder, and under it, I found a book—a book of spells, it turned out to be. I brought it in and read it, and…and that's when I found a spell called 'The Ultimate Cure.' That sounded just about right for how I was feeling at the time. If it was going to make my life worth living, then I was going to use it."

"What did it say?" Cam asked. "Didn't you know the spell would be dangerous?"

"That's just the point. The book didn't say what would happen if I used it. I had no idea the spell would create such a serious situation."

Wixer paced the floor and said, "If I'd known I was destroying the world, I would never have considered it." He sat on the side of his bed and hung his head so low that it almost disappeared between his shoulders. "All I wanted was to feel like I belonged. I really thought I'd feel better after doing the spell. Instead, I've been feeling sadder and sadder." He paused, "but I do feel a little better, being able to talk to all of you."

As dreadful as this revelation was, Cam still felt hopeful. "Maybe the spell book will tell us how to get rid of the Magician," Cam said.

With that plan, Wixer stood and retrieved the manual from under his mattress. Cam and Breem grabbed at the book and together poured through it, looking for answers—even one small hint of how they might be able to get rid of the Magician would be welcome. One by one, each had a turn hunting for a solution. Yet, their search failed to find a way to stop the spell and get rid of the Evil Magician.

Dwinda sighed and pushed the book away from her. "Then we'll have to continue on to Zarlock. He's our only answer now."

"Is that where you were going?" Wixer asked. "Then I simply must come with you. In my anger, I've done something very foolish. I must do whatever I can to make up for it."

"I'm not sure we need someone with such a bad temper," Cam said, regretting that he'd been the one to invite Wixer to join them.

If it was possible, Wixer's head sunk even lower. Speechless for a moment, Wixer said, "When I first saw you coming to my door, I thought just maybe you were the answer to the spell. Then you, Cam, asked me to come with you, and I began to hope I was right."

Breem cast a sharp glance at Cam. A slight shake of his head sent Cam a message that he should ease up on poor Wixer.

"Then again, I also thought it was strange," Wixer said. "No one has ever wanted me to join them before."

For a moment, there was no sound except a faint breeze whistling through the trees around Wixer's shack. "Now I know you didn't come as an answer to the spell," Wixer shrugged and looked toward the group. "I guess I don't deserve to come with you, but I'm the one who created this problem. I should be the one to help fix it."

Breem spoke up. "I think Wixer should come with us. He could help—plus, he'll see that he does have some friends in this world. Anyway," Breem said, looking straight at Cam, "haven't we all done things that we knew we shouldn't do?" Off to the side, Dwinda was nodding agreement with Breem's statement.

Breem's words hit their mark with Cam as he realized he was being too harsh. "That's true. If I can be dumb and walk into the

Moving Forest, then Wixer can make a mistake, too. Okay, Wixer, you're with us." Holding up his hand, he shouted, "High-five, dude."

Everyone stared at Cam, puzzled expressions on their faces. He just sat there, holding up his hand and grinning broadly into the quiet.

Gradually, the silence in the room caught his attention. "What?" he blurted out, examining each perplexed face.

"What exactly does 'high five dude' mean?" Dwinda asked.

Cam burst out laughing so hard tears rolled down his cheeks. He'd forgotten his new friends didn't know the customs of his world. Once he settled down, he reached for Wixer's hand, held it up, and then with his own, gave Wixer a high-five slap.

"When things are going good in my world, we give each other what we call 'high-five' because we have five fingers," he said, still grinning. "It's a sign that things are good." Turning to Wixer, he added, "In other words, Wixer, it would be great to have you join us."

Excited, Wixer jumped up and started giving everyone in the room high-fives. Before long, the whole room was filled with laughter as everyone, including Marvel, slapped each other's hands, wingtips, and other appendages in the air.

Chapter 18

The Rain

Late the next day, the small group found themselves trudging along the side of a wide canyon. Dwinda and Breem were in the lead, with Wixer and Cam following behind. Marvel soared with the wind out over the gorge. Cam looked at the hills on the other side of the ravine with the sun high in the cloudless Worpple sky as he walked. He was barely aware of the deep oranges, blues, and purples painted across the shadows of the canyon as thoughts of his own world crowded his mind.

By now, his family was probably worried about him. Perhaps they were searching for him at this very moment. He'd not only missed his visit with his father, but it was now Monday, a school day, and he was still not at home. What would they do when he returned with the fantastic story of his adventures in Worpple? Would they be angry or relieved that he was all right? He figured he deserved to have some punishment after disappearing for such a long time.

Wixer's deep voice at his side him pulled him out of his thoughts. "You're very quiet, Cam. You look unhappy, is anything wrong?"

"I missed my visit with Dad. I'm in real trouble now."

"Just explain it to them when you get back."

He knew if that were possible, things would be all right. But if he tried to explain his adventures in the cartoon world, he'd be in even worse trouble, and they would lock him up.

"Yeah, right, that oughta' do it. Wixer, they probably wouldn't believe me even if I took you home with me."

Pausing to pick up a long twig from the ground, he said, "I thought I hated where I live. Now that I may never see it again, it puts a whole new slant on things."

"Don't worry, little buddy, we'll get you out of this and safely home."

He saw the sincerity in Wixer's eyes and believed his newest friend would do his best to get everyone through this mess unharmed. Feeling a little better, he remembered, now that the big guy was joining them, he wasn't the only one able to fight whatever dangers came their way. Now the burden could be shared, and Cam felt a bit of the weight lift off his shoulders. Just then, his stomach made a loud rumble. "I'm starving! Are we gonna be eating soon?" he asked Breem and Dwinda who were ahead of him.

"We'll be stopping very soon," Dwinda said. "In fact, we couldn't have picked a better place to spend the night. The Tewins live a short distance from here, and it is perfect."

"What's so special about the Tewins?" he asked.

Just as Dwinda was about to answer, Breem interjected in a whisper and a smile. "Shhh, don't tell them, let it be a surprise."

"I don't really like surprises," Wixer said.

Dwinda, going along with Breem's suggestion, turned her head and looked at Wixer with a twinkle in her eyes. "Oh, you'll definitely like this one." Looking to Cam, she said, "I'll tell you this much, you absolutely do not have anything like the Tewins on your Earth."

Dwinda had no sooner finished speaking when the sky suddenly became dark and gloomy. Looking up, they saw deep black thunderclouds rolling over the land.

"Whoa!" exclaimed Cam. "Just a couple of minutes ago, the sky was completely clear. Now it looks like we're in for a..."

Before he finished his sentence, the sky opened up. It was as if a thousand sprinklers had all been turned on together.

"Run!" Dwinda pointed to a nearby umbrella tree.

Even though the tree kept them relatively dry, Cam was worried about standing under a tree during a storm. He knew that under a tree in a lightning storm was hazardous. But there was no lightning, so he relaxed and stayed with his friends.

From their shelter, the group watched the rain flow in enormous waves. In minutes, large puddles and small lakes were scattered everywhere.

"Does it always rain like this?" Cam asked over the din of the rain hitting the leaves above.

"Not that I've ever noticed," Breem shouted. "We get lots of rain, but I've never known it to come so suddenly or so hard before."

"Me neither," Dwinda said. "Strange indeed, in fact, there've been all sorts of bizarre things happening since we started this trip. I don't know what's going on. It's scary and difficult, not knowing what's going to happen next."

As quickly as it started, the storm ended, and the sun shone like a happy smile, giving the land a freshly washed appearance. The small group emerged from their shelter, and cheerfully wiped the water from their faces and arms.

The air was filled with an odor that made Cam think of happy days at home, and he tingled with energy. "That was awesome!" he shouted into the air. "I was worried it would last for hours and spoil our journey." A refreshing breeze sprang up from across the canyon, adding to the exhilarating feel. Cam felt the impulsive urge to run and feel the wind on his face. Running in large circles around the group, he threw his arms out as though he was a bird trying to take off. Then Cam straightened his course and went ahead of the others. He trotted along the path and felt exhilarated. "This is fun!" he shouted to the air.

While Dwinda watched Cam's exuberance, she cautioned him, "Don't get too far ahead. We'll be turning off this path soon."

At the exact moment, Dwinda was calling to Cam, he went to the edge of the canyon to see how deep it was. Invisible hands grabbed him from the air and shoved him over the cliff.

Chapter 19

The Cliff

Terrified, Cam yelled as he flew out into the air. He was sure he would fall forever into the bottomless pit below, and this time he really would die. He looked down into the deep ravine and knew there was no way he could be saved.

Scrambling, he grabbed at the branches and twigs that stuck out from the side of the canyon. But they were too wet from the recent flood of rain, and he couldn't get a grip. His hands slipped off as if they were coated with grease.

Just then, Cam felt a weird sensation—he was floating. The side of the canyon drifted by him as though he were a feather, drifting down, down, down. It felt like he could glide in the air like a bird or soar like a kite on the wind. As he settled downward, he had the impression he was being buoyed up by an invisible force. He neared a ledge jutting out from the side of the gorge. As he got closer, his body seemed to hover in the air before being gently placed on the projecting shelf.

Anxiously, he checked himself all over and was delighted to find not a single injury. His landing had been so soft he might as well have fallen on a pile of raked leaves. Slowly, he got to his feet, rubbed the gooseflesh on his upper arms, and considered himself lucky. In this strange land, he didn't stop to wonder what had caused him to float rather than tumble down the steep cliff. He shrugged and accepted it as just another strange event that happened in this weird world of Worpple. He looked up, trying to see how he could climb to the top of the cliff.

When Cam went over the edge of the cliff, Marvel screamed an enormous "Whoop!" and flew out into the canyon. Then she watched as he floated onto the protruding shelf.

Seeing Cam disappear, Wixer raced to the edge of the canyon and looked down. There on the ledge stood his pal covered with mud.

"Are you okay, little buddy?"

"Yeah!" Cam shouted back. "Nothing's broken, and I don't see any blood, so I guess I'm okay."

Looking up, he saw two more heads as Breem and Dwinda joined Wixer's over the cliff to peer down at him. Suddenly he remembered the feel of invisible hands that had come out of the void and pushed him over the cliff. "Hey, get back!" he warned. "Somebody pushed me from there!"

Having no encounters with the Evil Magician, Wixer couldn't figure out what he was talking about. "Huh? There wasn't anyone near him."

Breem opened his mouth to explain to Wixer when Dwinda interrupted. "We have to get him out of there. We'll explain everything."

Everyone became active in the effort to get Cam back up. First, he tried climbing, but the ground was covered with mud from the sudden rain, and each time he gained a bit, he slipped back down.

Marvel then tried to carry him, but Cam was much too heavy for her, even with his help.

Next, Dwinda proposed they rip apart the bedding and make a long rope to throw down to him. That idea was rejected because it would ruin the linen, and they would have nothing to sleep on. Besides, it would take too long if the Evil Magician was lurking around.

Breem thought of climbing down but changed his mind when he

saw how slippery the mud was. Then the group would have two of them to save.

Finally, Wixer came up with the best idea. Lying on his stomach, he reached down to Cam with a long branch that everyone had rubbed dry. Breem and Dwinda sat on Wixer's back to keep him from slipping down the edge of the cliff. While Cam held onto the branch, he used his feet to pull himself up the ridge, Wixer pulled, and Marvel held Cam's T-shirt and helped hoist him to the top. The joint effort paid off. It wasn't long before Cam scaled the cliff and rejoined his friends.

He was no sooner at the top when Wixer asked, "Now, what do you mean you were pushed? I never saw anyone near you. Who pushed you?"

"I know who!" Breem shouted, as Dwinda gave an agreeing nod. "It was that Evil Magician."

"That's right," Cam said, as he stood covered with mud. His voice became hushed. "Creepy man—he's here right now—I can feel him."

Wixer spun around, searching the air for traces of the sinister presence. "Where is he? I brought him here, and I want to be the one to eliminate him."

The Evil Magician's sinister laughter filled the air as his caped form materialized. "Thank you, Wixer. Your stupidity has given me life again. I was asleep for a very, very long time." His eyes glared at Wixer. "So, you think you can get rid of me single-handed. I see you do not yet realize the power I wield—I will demonstrate momentarily."

Strutting, he addressed Cam. "Your luck has saved you again, I see. I enjoyed watching everyone's efforts to save you. That rainstorm was a great idea on my part, don't you think? I was hoping you would fall to the bottom, and if not, that you would never be able to get back up that slippery slope."

Breem, Dwinda, and Marvel huddled together off to one side. Their eyes shone with terror and worry. Wixer stood near his Earth friend, ready to attack should his strength be needed. Cam stood about a yard back from the Evil Magician and impending danger.

With a terrible hissing yell, the Evil Magician pointed his claw-like finger at Cam. A great blue-ray sprang from his hand and sped toward the boy as though he were a target in a video game.

Everything seemed to move in slow motion as Cam stood paralyzed, unable to stop what was about to happen. Just as the menacing ray was about to smash into the cringing boy, it mysteriously split into two beams that passed around him as though he had an invisible shield protecting him. Cam watched in astonishment as the horrible ray flowed around his body instead of through him. He was left unharmed and wondering what was happening.

"I will get you," the Evil Magician shrieked, sounding like Cam the day he was forced off the field by Jason and his gang. "I will get you, even if I have to take all these sordid supporters around you too."

Here, the similarity with Cam ended as the villain turned to Breem and Dwinda, shoved his ugly face close to them, and hissed. "Leave! Leave while you still have a chance, or I will be forced to destroy you too." With these words, the Evil Magician faded from view.

The hair on the back of Cam's neck stood up like sentinels on guard. Now the Evil Magician was threatening to kill his friends as well. As he looked at the others, he was filled with outrage. How dare that magician threaten his friends if they stayed with him. That sounded too much like what Jason was doing back home with the science project. At that moment, his resolve hardened—he was going to complete this trip and win. Meanwhile, whatever it took to ensure the safety of the others, he would do.

Wixer and Dwinda stood as still as statues in shock and disbelief.

"What happened?" Wixer asked. "How come that ray didn't kill you? And how come you weren't hurt falling over that cliff?"

"I don't know," Cam said, equally confused and concerned. His shoulders hunched in toward his chest as he stared at the ground.

"I think I know," Breem said. "It was the Madra Stone. It's protecting you, Cam."

"A Madra Stone—what's that?" Wixer asked.

"Whoop," Marvel said, agreeing with Wixer's curiosity.

"It's a stone I found in the woods," he said as he yanked it out of his pocket. "It's magic, and it's saved my life twice now."

As everyone gathered around to look at the magnificent glowing stone, Cam brightened up and exclaimed, "You're right, Breem—I forgot all about it. This Madra Stone will help all of us get through this trip safely. I don't know how, but I'm going to do all I can to bring its protection to all of you as well."

He eased the stone into his pocket. "Let's hurry. The sooner we get to Zarlock, the better."

Chapter 20

The Tewins

The group stood near a short hedge that surrounded the Tewin compound. Nature decorated the shrubbery with beautiful, enormous, multi-colored flowers that grew in profusion and filled the air with sweet fragrance.

Standing quietly, the travelers watched several odd little creatures scurry about their settlement. The tallest was only about four feet. Their pear-shaped bodies were covered with soft, multi-colored fur with flexible penguin-like arms.

How they managed to walk was something of a mystery to the observers. It was difficult to tell if they even had feet. The stubby, round appendages were covered with a full ruff of fur. This feature made the Tewins amusing to watch. As they wobbled around, they bumped and stumbled into things—bushes, houses, and even each other. Still, this did not deter them from their various activities. They alternated between bouncing off whatever was near them and scurrying about in quick little movements. The scene delighted the visitors—even Wixer could not keep a smile off his face.

The same thick fur that covered their feet also formed a fringe around their necks. The Tewins' heads were round, like their bodies, with pointed noses and pouted mouths. The tops of their flat heads curved out over their foreheads like a built-in umbrella.

Cam was most fascinated by the Tewins' heads. They swiveled around in a full circle, often making it difficult for others to know if they were coming or going. This ability also enhanced their clumsiness. As they traveled in one direction, they looked in another, inevitably bumping and bobbing into each other.

"These guys are too funny. I see what you mean, Dwinda." Cam chuckled. "We definitely don't have anything like this in my world."

"Yes, they are amusing." Dwinda giggled. "They are such friendly and happy creatures. I was especially looking forward to this part of the trip."

Just then, one of the Tewins noticed the travelers standing at the edge of their settlement. He scampered up to the group while calling out to the others in a high-pitched elf-like voice. "Visitors! Look, we have visitors! Come on, let's go talk to them."

"Yes," cried another, "we can find out who they are."

Before long, curious Tewins encircled the travelers, all talking at once in their elf voices. If Cam closed his eyes, he would be sure he was caught in the middle of the movie, *The Wonderful Wizard of Oz.*
"Hello. Who are you?" the first Tewin asked.

"Look. they have whooper with them," a blue one said to his friend.

"I heard it's good luck when a whooper comes to call," the orange Tewin said.

"Did you come far?" asked a squeaky female voice.

"Would you like to put your feet up?" a green Tewin asked as he rushed to catch up.

"You could stay at my house tonight if you want," another one said.

"Hey. Let me see. You're standing in my way," a short purple Tewin said as she shoved her way to the front.

One turned to his friend and said, "That hairy guy sure is big. Are you a giant?" he asked.

The last comment was directed at Wixer. Before he could answer, a distinguished-looking Tewin noisily wobbled down the street. He was decked out in an official ribbon and medallion. If it were possible, he looked even a little more rotund than the other Tewins. As he came huffing and puffing up to them, he called, "Wait for me! Wait for me!" The visitors soon discovered he was the Tewin mayor.

The mayor's green body emphasized his sparkling orange eyes that were also fixed on Wixer. Nervously, he began his official welcome, in his best authoritative, elfin voice. "Welcome to Tewinville."

He paused to clean his glasses and place them back on his nose, and then a broad smile spread across his face as he recognized two of the visitors. "Why, it's Dwinda and Breem. How nice of you to come to visit us. We enjoyed your last stay so much."

"We were delighted to be coming here," Breem said as he stepped out of the group. "We brought some friends with us this time." Turning to Wixer, Cam, and Marvel, Breem introduced them.

"Wonderful, wonderful," the mayor said. "We're always thrilled to have company. This is even better, though, because some old friends have also arrived. Welcome to Tewinville, everyone."

"This time, we're passing through on official business," Dwinda said. "We're going to see Zarlock."

"Well, upon my wobbly body, is it important? Or are you having another adventure, Breem?" Without waiting for an answer, he said, "Please, everyone, come to my house for some refreshments and tell me all about it."

The Tewins' houses were dome-shaped, like an upside-down bowl placed on the ground. The doorways, flush with the building, were high enough for the Tewins to pass through. Cam and Breem had to bend down to enter, and Breem had to squeeze his fat tummy through the small opening into the mayor's house. Not so for poor Wixer. He was a foot taller than his friends and more expansive than everyone else. He tried to crawl in on his hands and knees and...

"Help! I'm stuck. I can't move," a distressed Wixer bellowed.

And so he was.

It wasn't until later in the day that Cam and Breem fully understood the events that followed and both sides of what happened.

Now Cam and Breem were on the inside with Wixer's head and shoulders while Dwinda, Marvel, the mayor, and the rest of Tewinville were on the outside with Wixer's back end.

Even though Wixer's head was right there beside him, and Breem could have spoken to Wixer, he turned to Cam instead. "We'll have to push him out. If we pull him in, we'll never get him out again, so push."

On the outside, the mayor gave directions. "He wants to get in, so shove him."

Cam and Breem, on the inside, pushed and pushed. Dwinda, Marvel, and the Tewins on the outside also pushed and pushed. Cam couldn't figure out why poor Wixer wasn't moving.

All the while, Wixer yelled, "The wrong way, the other way!"

"I guess he wants to come in after all—pull!" Breem said to Cam.

At the same time, Dwinda turned to everyone on the outside and said, "It sounds like he wants to come out—pull!"

Once more, those on the outside were pulling and pulling, while inside, Cam and Breem were also pulling and pulling.

Again, Wixer started bellowing, "No, no! That's wrong, the other way!"

Finally, with his hands on his hips, Breem stood in front of Wixer's face and asked, "Just what do you want, Wixer?"

Wixer yelled, "I want out of here."

Meanwhile, on the outside, a helpful Tewin suggested, "Maybe we should wet him. That will make him slippery, and he'll come out more easily."

A second Tewin didn't think that was such a good idea. "Well, that might have worked that time when Binker got stuck in Jutt's fence, but it didn't work when Mar got stuck in the tree. No, I think we'll just have to break the door apart."

The Tewin mayor didn't think much of this suggestion. It was, after all, his door. "Grease him! That always works," he said.

A couple of Tewins ran off to get some butter and a ladder. Before long, everyone on the outside was busy greasing Wixer. Once he was well-buttered, one and all again prepared to free him from his bondage.

"Now, let's get this straight; you want out, right?" asked Breem before the pushing or pulling started.

"Yes!" Wixer cried.

Again, the great effort began. Fortunately, this time the inside pushed, and those outside pulled, and Wixer popped out with a "splunk."

Chapter 21

The Feast

The Tewin's made a great fuss over Wixer.

"Oh, dear." the mayor cried. "Are you all right?" He brushed at the giant with a handkerchief.

While Wixer sat on the ground, two-dozen Tewins buzzed around and created a great racket. They chattered together as they scrubbed the butter from Wixer's sides. In all the noise they were making, it was impossible to know what each was saying—several called out to each other. Two more hauled away the ladder and complained about the weight. Half a dozen more talked about making plans in honor of the company.

"Hey buddy, are you okay? Cam shouted to project his voice over the din.

Once most of the butter was cleaned off, Wixer sat quietly, checking his body for injuries. "Yes, I'm fine," he said.

When all had calmed down, the mayor said, "You can stay at our meetinghouse. Even Wixer can get through that door."

The mayor was right. Wixer had no trouble fitting through the meetinghouse's double doorway, although he did have to crawl to get in. Once inside, visitors and residents all found a comfortable place to sit and listen. Cam and his friends sat on the floor as the chairs were too small and delicate to handle their weight and size. They told the mayor of the evil that had invaded their world and their adventures along the way.

Understandably, the mayor was upset by the news. Throughout the land, the Tewins were known for their exceptional generosity and kindness. It was not a surprise to Dwinda and Breem when, with a grand flourish, the mayor rose from his seat, stretching himself as tall as his four feet would allow. Then, holding a pointed finger up toward the ceiling, he vowed, "I promise that we will do whatever we can to help in any way." The other Tewins chattered all at once, voicing their agreement with their mayor.

"Thank you, Mayor," Dwinda smiled. "We will let you know what you can do if we need your help."

Quietly Cam watched the funny little creatures. As he listened to what was being said, sadness gripped him. He thought about the horror invading their world. Cam could not imagine how these loving little beings could win over the Evil Magician. The Tewins were what that sinister creature was working to destroy. Not for the first time, he again vowed to himself he would protect the good and noble beings he met in Worpple. The problem was he had no idea how this would be accomplished, or even if he could do it.

Once the meeting was over, the travelers were led to the river to bathe. Wixer busied himself scrubbing the remaining butter from his sides while Cam washed out the mud, caked on his clothing, hair, and skin, from the fall over the cliff. The bath felt magnificent—he had never realized how pleasing getting clean could be. Since arriving in Worpple, Cam had been wearing the same clothes. With extra care, he took a few minutes to give them a scrub as well. When he was finished, he felt fresh and clean as if he had washed off the Evil Magician's contamination.

While the group was occupied with their meeting and bath, the remaining Tewins created a delicious banquet for everyone. By the time the travelers were heading back to the meetinghouse, Cam's stomach was rumbling. He thought he was hungry back when they were on the path to the Tewins' village. However, when they ate, he reasoned even the Brussels sprouts and liver his mother pushed at him would have been welcome.

The banquet was worth the wait when it finally came. All of Tewinville crowded into the meetinghouse, and an enormous feast of bizarre food was offered to the visitors. It was a welcome change from the berries, cheese, and bread that Dwinda had brought.

Recounting the feast later, Cam could not say what exactly he'd eaten. Some things reminded him of tacos and sauce. Yet, the sauce was not spicy; it was sweet. There was something similar to berry soup and crispy bread. He liked best, though, a dish that looked like pasta but tasted like a hamburger. When he told Breem what he thought of the pasta-like recipe, Breem informed him that it was a vegetable grown locally.

That evening the travelers snuggled down to sleep near a fireplace that had been lit as the evening grew colder. Marvel was nestled close to Cam as he began to drift into sleep.

The silence was broken by Breem's hollow voice. "By this time tomorrow, we'll have completed our task."

"That is if we aren't stopped by the Orbins," Dwinda said.

As close to sleep as Cam had been, he propped himself up on his elbow and asked, "What are you talking about? Who, or what, are the Orbins?"

"I think they're a bunch of thieves who live in the Jampar forest," Wixer said to Cam and turned to look at Dwinda. "But I don't understand. Why should we worry about them?"

"The Tewin mayor told me they've decided to take over the forest. They won't allow anyone to go through without some kind of payment," she said. "But that's the only way to Zarlock, so we really don't have a choice. Let's hope that if we run into them and they hear how serious the situation is that they'll be willing to listen to reason."

"Just let me at them, I'll show them who's boss," Wixer said, sounding tough.

"I know you're powerful, Wixer," said Dwinda, "but there are lots of them and only five of us. We'd better be prepared in case the Orbins aren't willing to use common sense."

Cam sat right up in his blanket and disturbed Marvel, cuddled next to him. "Oh man, these Orbin characters sound like some creeps I know from my world. Nothing would please me more than to wipe up the ground with Jason and his pals."

"I sure hope we won't have to 'wipe up the ground' with the Orbins," Breem said.

Dwinda sat up and looked at Cam. "You should be okay. You have the Madra Stone. Remember, it's already protected you a couple of times."

"His stone may protect him, but it won't help us," Breem said. "The Magician has threatened to kill us if we continue to stick with Cam."

Wixer softly snored as the others pondered their dilemma.

"Don't come unglued guys," Cam said. "I'll do whatever I can to make sure we all make it to Zarlock safely. See you in the morning." He snuggled down once more with Marvel and soon drifted off to sleep.

Just beyond the Tewin settlement, at the back of the meetinghouse, a dark shadow lingered. "So, the brat from Earth has a Madra Stone," the Evil Magician said. "I must get that stone away from the boy, although...I may have to enlist the help of these Orbin characters."

Without his usual evil laugh, the Evil Magician faded into the night. "Thanks for the valuable information, Cam—I'll see you at the Orbin camp."

Chapter 22

The Orbins

The sun poked its ruby head above the horizon as the group left the Tewin village. Brilliant streaks of red, purple, and orange spread across the sky like playful fingers dancing in the golden light. As everyone walked in a staggered line, Breem and Dwinda didn't seem to notice the glorious spectacle the sunrise was painting for them. They'd been very quiet as they ate the morning meal and prepared for the day's journey. Cam was uncomfortable with Breem's quietness. It was strange compared to his usual playful nature.

As if to distract all thoughts of their plight ahead, Wixer stopped and looked up at the sky's display. "It's hard to imagine that trouble could be waiting when you see beauty such as this."

Dwinda and Breem looked up at the sky and, with a grunt, continued walking, their heads down and their shoulders hunched. They were too lost in their thoughts to pay attention to the sunrise.

Cam stopped to take in the stunning sight with his friend. "You're right, Wixer. It does seem out of place that we could have problems with this beauty all around us; they just don't seem to mix." The thought of trouble soon had Cam's mind deeply engrossed in his own thoughts.

The Evil Magician wouldn't be able to survive in my world. He stroked Marvel. "It's not a total disaster," he said to his friends. "If we can't stop the Magician, we'll just send everyone from here over to my world. Earth's got some mighty scary weapons. There's no way the Magician could take over that world."

Breem smiled at his friend, "That's so considerate, Cam, but it isn't that simple. We don't have enough openings to get everyone, or everything, like the Gigglewits, to a new world. And even if we did, it's an enormous task that could take years."

"Then there's the Earth's ecology," Dwinda said. "We don't know if Julie, for example, would survive in your polluted environment."

"Hold it," Cam cried. "We could create a special environment for Julie and the rest of you, for that matter. We might even be able to create other openings."

"Are you serious?" Wixer asked. "Your world knows how to do that?"

"I'm not joking. We absolutely can create the environment because we've already done that for other situations. I'm not exactly sure about the new openings, but I bet we probably could do it once we figured out how they work."

"How amazing!" Breem said, "I knew your world was more advanced than ours, but I had no idea they could do things like that." He stooped down and plucked a blade of grass from the ground. As he played with it in his hand, he said, "I must confess, I've been having visions of our world completely dead with nothing left but the Evil Magician and his criminal behavior."

"Not in my lifetime," Cam said. "But one of you would have to come back with me to help explain this world."

"Thanks a lot, Cam," Dwinda said as she patted him on the back.

"It's good to know there's a backup plan, although I sure hope we never have to use it."

As usual, Dwinda and Breem directed the way for the small group while Cam and Wixer followed. Marvel occasionally flew off with cheerful "whoops" over the land. Moments later, she returned to make happy loops in the air. Then she would repeat her excursions all over again.

A few hours later, the group spotted the Jampar Forest across the plain in the distance. With eyes twinkling, Breem turned to Dwinda. "Is it time to eat yet?"

"When we get a little closer to the forest, it will be a perfect time to eat." Dwinda laughed.

"Oh boy, this is the time I've been waiting for," Breem said, throwing a playful punch at Cam's arm. "Now we get to have all those left-over goodies from the Tewins' feast."

"Let's go for it." Cam cheered.

The group's pace picked up as they sprinted across the field, and soon everyone was digging into the food in enjoyment. Cam and Wixer shared their food with Marvel. In turn, she rolled in the air to show her joy.

Not far from where the small group gathered, two Orbins watched from their lookout post in the forest trees.

The sight of Cam and Wixer feeding and stroking a whooper greatly amused the Orbins in the tree. "Huh, look at dat!" The first Orbin snarled as he shoved a branch out of his line of vision.

"Dem guys is feedin' a whooper. Only sucky babies is good ta whoopers. So deys gotta be wimps, dat's fer sure."

"You got it, pal," his companion agreed. "Our guys is gonna take 'em easy. Come on, let's go tell da boss."

Together the Orbins hurried down from the tree and skulked off into the woods to inform the others.

Vit, the leader, enjoyed sunning himself on a quiet afternoon when the Orbins from the outlook rushed up to him. "Boss!" the first one yelled.

"Dis better be good," Vit said, barely raising his head from the arm it was resting on. "I was gettin' ready fer a nap."

"They's a bunch o' wimps what's comin' ta pass through da

forest," Snoops, the second Orbin, said.

"Is dat, right?" Vit smiled his wolfish grin. "Well, in dat case, come on, gang, let's go!" Speaking first to the lookout keepers and then to two others nearby, Vit said, "Youse guys all come with me. The rest of youse get into yer positions."

Chapter 23

The Fight

Cam rolled on the ground with Marvel. He had a slice of bread and berries that Marvel wanted. Between the whooping and the laughter, it was hard to see who was getting the worst of the deal. Suddenly, Marvel stopped playing and flew straight up into the air with a tremendous, "WHOOP." Flapping her wings, she dashed away, screeching all the way.

"Why'd she do that?" Cam asked, mystified.

"The Orbins are here!" Dwinda said as she rushed to gather the few articles on the ground left from their lunch. The group gazed toward the forest and the small gang of Orbins at its edge.

"What's the big fuss?" Cam whispered to Breem. "They're small, and there are only five of them. We can take 'em easy."

"Don't be fooled by their size," Breem said. "They can be vicious fighters.

While they ate their meal, Dwinda told Cam about the Orbins. "They are green, slimy creatures," she said. A shiver ran through her as she spoke. "They're about four feet tall and their bodies are covered with loose skin that is like loose melted goo oozing all over their bodies.

Orbin's heads are round and hairless with ball-like eyes and enormous, pointed ears that stick out like flags on the side of their skulls."

"They really are repulsive," Breem said. "They have wolf-like snouts with large purple fangs jutting out from their upper and lower jaws. Their arms and legs are muscular and powerful with long, sharp purple claws capable of ripping a foe to shreds.

Dwinda smiled at Breem in agreement with what he was telling Cam. "That's true, she said. "Orbins had no qualms about hurting anyone to get what they want. They will do anything to anyone, even their friends, at any time. Orbins are so cold-hearted, they actually enjoy hurting others."

That's right," Breem said. "Especially when they think they are weak. Causing pain to those who can't fight back is a great sport just to hear them squeal.

Vit took great pleasure in detailing what he wanted to do to Cam and his friends. As he proudly strutted up and down in front of his gang, he hissed, "I was gonna take dem guys by surprise. But da stupid whooper killed dat idea, so we hast'a come up with somethin' differ'nt."

Stopping in front of two Orbins, he said, "Snoop an' Markle, I thought youse said dey was a bunch of wimps. Good ting our plans is delayed," Vit boasted as he stared out into the clearing at the travelers. "It's a piece o' cake takin' da fat, blue one an' da green one. But I don't like da looks o' dem other two. Da big one's a mean sucker an' I never seen da likes o' da other one."

"But boss,' Snoops said, "dems da ones what was feedin' and pattin' da whooper."

"Well." Vit brightened. "Dat puts another slant on it." A big smile spread across his face and formed a grimace of purple teeth. "One ting's fer sure, we gotta get 'em into da woods so's we's got a real good chance at 'em."

The travelers were also examining the handful of Orbins just as the foul creatures were discussing how they had a "real good chance at 'em." Seeing no aggressive actions coming in their direction, first Wixer, then Cam carefully approached the band. Following behind, at a much slower pace, were Breem and Dwinda. Marvel was nowhere to be seen.

Watching their approach, Vit said in his raspy, contemptuous voice, “Hey guys! Deys comin’ ta make us rich—ain’t dat just grand?” Then Vit stuck out his chest in pride. After all, it had been his idea to charge those going through the forest.

Vit took great pleasure in detailing what he wanted to do to Cam and his friends. As he proudly strutted up and down in front of his gang, he hissed, “I was gonna take dem guys by surprise. But da stupid whooper killed dat idea, so we hast’a come up with somethin’ differ’nt.”

Stopping in front of two Orbins, he said, “Snoop an’ Markle, I thought youse said dey was a bunch of wimps. Good ting our plans is delayed,” Vit boasted as he stared out into the clearing at the travelers. “It’s a piece o’ cake takin’ da fat, blue one an’ da green one. But I don’t like da looks o’ dem other two. Da big one’s a mean sucker an’ I never seen da likes o’ da other one.”

“But boss,’ Snoops said, “dems da ones what was feedin’ and pattin’ da whooper.”

“Well.” Vit brightened. “Dat puts another slant on it.” A big smile spread across his face and formed a grimace of purple teeth. “One ting’s fer sure, we gotta get ’em into da woods so’s we’s got a real good chance at ’em.”

The travelers were also examining the handful of Orbins just as the foul creatures were discussing how they had a “real good chance at ’em.” Seeing no aggressive actions coming in their direction, first Wixer, then Cam carefully approached the band. Following behind, at a much slower pace, were Breem and Dwinda. Marvel was nowhere to be seen.

Watching their approach, Vit said in his raspy, contemptuous voice, “Hey guys! Deys comin’ ta make us rich—ain’t dat just grand?” Then Vit stuck out his chest in pride. After all, it had been his idea to charge those going through the forest.

Chapter 24

The Camp

Lashed with thick vines, the travelers looked more like Lego sets chained together than peaceful voyagers on a critical mission. A sturdy vine was laced around their waist, and their hands were tied behind their backs. The vine was then strung from the back of one prisoner to the next until they created a string of hostages. Dwinda and Breem came first, followed by Cam and Wixer.

They were led down a narrow path that wandered through the forest. Low hanging branches and vines scratched at their faces and bodies. At the same time, their captors pushed and shoved them as they made their way to the camp.

"Wanna bet dat big one's gonna make the loudest noise?"

The travelers could hear the Orbins discussing them from behind.

"Yeah?" A second, Orbin asked. "Well, I thinks it's gonna be da fat blue guy. He sure looks like a wimp ta me."

"Yer both wrong," a third voice said. "I thinks it's gonna be that strange creature what's got the weird orange hair."

All the way, Cam and his friends were taunted by their captors. They were making bets over which of them was going to squeal the loudest when they were hurt.

The Orbin camp was a circle of straw huts with a bonfire in the middle. Old logs were placed around the fire to offer the beasts a place to sit. To one side, wooden poles were deeply embedded into the ground and stood about two feet apart. It didn't take the Orbins long to harshly lash their prisoners to these poles.

Cam felt so sad and miserable that he could barely hold his head up. He had promised his friends he would protect them from danger with his Madra Stone. Yet here they were in this mess. Anxious for them, he looked at his companions and wondered what good his Madra Stone was right now. Was he supposed to do something to activate it? Tied to the pole as he was, there wasn't much he was able to do. How come the stone saved his life the time he fell over the cliff and not this time? How were he and his friends going to get out of this disaster? As Dwinda had pointed out, things may be okay for him with the stone, but it didn't mean he could use it for them. It had to work for his friends because it wouldn't mean much if they never make it.

He thought of the lessons Julie shared with him. As he remembered his connection with the life force, he began to feel a little better. Then Cam realized that he also shared the same life force with these beautiful friends. And while he really didn't want to think about it, he also realized that the same life force was also in the Orbins. After all, they were a life form just like the rest of them.

As Cam gave himself a little shake and pulled himself away from his thoughts, he noticed Dwinda's and Breem's attention was riveted on Wixer. Vit and two Orbins were standing on a wooden box in front of his friend. Each wielded a long, thin, evil-looking knife. The sharp blades flashed in the light, and Cam could see dried blood stuck to the edge. His imagination raced through all the scary movies he had seen as he tried to imagine where the blood had come from.

"First, we's gonna chop off those antennee on yer head." Vit waved his knife under Wixer's nose. "Then we's gonna start at yer toes an' work up. Okay, boys; get rid o' those things on top o' his head."

As an Orbin reached up to grab Wixer's feelers, a sudden loud scream slashed the air. Twirling toward the sound, Vit and the travelers realized the forest was a solid sheet of flames. Vit and his men dropped their knives and joined the other Orbins that were deserting the area.

Chapter 25

The Fire

Cam watched in horror as the fire, like a wicked monster on a computer game, rapidly swallowed up the trees around the camp. Until now, everything he had seen in this world had been like a three-dimensional cartoon movie. Yet the fire that now roared just yards away looked like a normal fire in his world. Flames reached toward the sky and danced in the air like a dizzy ballerina before leaping onto another branch.

His skin crawled with fear. Hot air engulfed the travelers in a gray and dismal shroud. Just then, the air shimmered in the now-familiar entrance of the Magician. Soon, the malicious entity stood before them, his head thrown back in a roar of glee.

"Did you really think you could escape from me?" The Evil Magician asked, his hot sticky breath just inches away from Cam's face. "Your Madra Stone will be of no use to you now. Finally, I've got you where I want you."

To the others, he shouted, "You were warned not to help the Earth boy, but you would not listen. Now you will pay!"

He spun around and pointed his finger toward the Orbins' straw huts. Flames jumped from his finger and engulfed the dwellings. Within seconds, the whole area flashed like the wild lights of a carnival marquee.

The evil beast turned back to the four travelers, a fierce grin on his face. The danger was clear to the captives—the flames would reach their wooden posts soon. There would be no hope then.

"You will all be roasted!" the Magician screamed.

Cam shuddered as he listened to the sinister, hideous laughter.

"At last, I am free to take over this world. After hundreds of years of exile, I will be the ultimate ruler."

The Magician glared at Cam and his friends. "What a shame I cannot witness your torture. I see the fire is beginning to spread onto the grass. Since I do not want to share your fate, I must leave you now." His diabolic laughter lingered as he left.

Cam sat transfixed as he watched the harsh flames move closer and closer. Dread pounded in every nerve ending. The terror was so overpowering it felt like his life was being choked out of him. A scream formed in his throat.

Just then, Marvel's cries filled the air as she soared into view. With a swoop, she flew down to where Cam was tied to the pole. Oblivious to the danger, she worked at the restraints holding him with her claws. The fire inched closer. Scalding heat reached for him as he felt the vines loosen around his body.

With a cry, Marvel sprang into the air and headed for Breem. Cam, in turn, rushed to Wixer to free him. He thought of using the knives left by the Orbins, but the mere thought of touching those vile implements sent shivers of disgust through him. Moments later, the whole group was unshackled. Once loose from the vines, Dwinda fell to the ground, coughing and grasping at her throat.

The air was thick with smoke. There was no way out. Smoke stung Cam's eyes, his lungs. Heat scorched his flesh.

There has to be a way out of this. What was it that Julie tried to tell him? He had a life-power within him he could use in times of crisis. *But does fire have the same life force as living things?* No time to worry about that now. Just do it. Closing his eyes, he thought of his own life force. Then he tried to see that same element within the fire. He opened his eyes. Nothing. The fire had advanced even closer.

At that moment, he felt the warmth from his pocket. He pulled out his Madra Stone to see that it glowed intensely in a swirl of color with arcing sparks of energy spewing out. It was like nothing he had ever seen before. Shoving it back into his pocket, he worked to hold up a still-struggling Dwinda. Was it his imagination? Had the grass fire moved back to a safe distance from them?

Holding Dwinda under her arms as she coughed and gasped, he glanced up toward the forest and then blinked to take a second look. A large tunnel had formed in the sea of smoke and flame. Was it his imagination? No, sure enough, an open archway appeared before them to escape through.

"This way!" shouted Cam. Soon the whole group fled through a gap in the flames and smoke to safety.

As Cam and Dwinda dashed out of the blaze, he felt a splash of water on his face. Gently he let go of his friend and looked up. Cam had expected to see rain. Instead, he was greeted by one of the strangest scenes he had ever witnessed.

Flying above him were enormous green and purple creatures. Their bodies were shaped like giant sea horses, with immense dragonfly-like wings attached to their bodies. Each one had filled itself with water and now sprayed at the fire through their mouths. The sky was a swarming mass of green and purple as it was filled with strange beings. In waves, they came until, at last, the fire was extinguished.

"Wow! What are they?" Cam asked.

"That's the Stoflie." Breem beamed. "Marvel must have gone for them. You'll be talking to them soon."

"Those things can talk? Fantastic." Cam was delighted until he gave the situation a second thought. "Now, why should that surprise me?" He laughed. "After all, I'm standing here talking to a big, blue creature from a cartoon dimension."

While everyone seemed safe, Wixer looked worried. "We should get out of here, but I don't know how," he said. "In the excitement, we got twisted around. One way looks about the same as any other in the forest."

"Oh, that's easy," Breem said confidently, "just follow the Stoflie. They're going in the same direction we're heading."

"That's right," Dwinda said, now recovered from the effects of the fire. "We learned that the last time we were here." The conversation then bounced back and forth between the two friends. "When Breem and I were here the last time, we got twisted around."

"That's right," Breem said. "Although we didn't have any problems with the Orbins that time."

"They weren't charging to go through the woods then and pretty much left us alone."

"So, our trip was fairly quiet and almost peaceful. Except—we got confused while traveling through this forest." Breem nodded at Dwinda.

"Eventually, when we thought we were completely lost, we noticed these wonderful creatures flying above us. They called down to us to follow them."

"They led us out of the forest and in the right direction to Zarlock." Breem grinned.

With a final glance up before moving on, Cam saw there were still a few Stoflie in the air. Although the fire seemed to be out, they continued to bring water to spray the smoldering branches. Turning to Wixer with a grin, he was even more delighted to see his friend had saved all their bundles. Everything had been recovered.

"Cool, Wixer," Cam cried. "You got our stuff." Everyone crowded around Wixer with gratitude and retrieved their load.

Once again, the group marched toward their destination. Cam watched his friends work their way through the forest. They had only been traveling for three days, and yet, it felt like they had known each other for months, perhaps even years. He couldn't imagine letting anything terrible happen to them. He cared for them too much.

It didn't take long before they arrived at a river, the last hurdle to reach Zarlock. Each one flopped down on the purple grass-covered ground in exhaustion.

"Cam," Dwinda said, giving him a big hug, "you're a hero. You saved our lives."

He wasn't ready to accept all the credit. He knew how close it had been. "Not I," he said as he passed Dwinda's hug on to Marvel. Rubbing the soft fur on her head, he said, "Marvel, you're the real hero. I don't think I can ever thank you enough."

"Whooop," Marvel said softly.

"How much longer?" Cam asked as he rested with his companions.

"We're almost at Zarlock's." Breem smiled. "We don't need to worry now."

"Well, I need a rest," Wixer said.

"I'm with you," Dwinda said.

While the group sat by the river soaking up the sun's energy, Cam turned to Dwinda and said, "So, tell me about Zarlock. What's he like? What does he do?"

"A Zarlock is someone who's been appointed by all the inhabitants of Worpple. We have a nomination process that goes to a special panel that selects the next Zarlock. Usually, this is just a formality because most of us know who the next Zarlock will be."

Breem said, "It's the person who has been the wisest and done the most for Worpple. Once a Zarlock is named, he or she then has that role for life, unless that person is too ill to continue."

Pausing to suck the sweet juice from some purple grass, Dwinda said, "From what I've learned, the Zarlocks of the past have spent most of their time meditating. And that's also true of the one we have now. He's getting quite old and doesn't pay much attention to time. He eats when he wants, collects food when he's out, and sleeps when he's tired. Someday, I would like to be appointed a Zarlock," Dwinda said.

"Would you? Wow, that'd be cool. Good luck. So, how do I talk to him?" Cam asked as he leaned back on his elbows. "Do I call him 'Your Honor' or 'Your Majesty' or what?"

Breem and Wixer smiled at Cam's question. Dwinda too found it amusing and said, "Just call him Zarlock. He's warm and friendly. I don't think he'd be comfortable with a title. Just treat him with respect."

Chapter 26

The Agreement

A short distance from the travelers stood some cliffs with a series of caves tunneled into their sides. Within one of these caves, the unhappy Orbins were gathered. They had fled the fire. Anger and disappointment crowded the cavern. One Orbin expressed his frustration as he advanced menacingly toward Vit.

"A big mess, dat's what. Yer big ideas ain't got us nowheres but trouble. Now we ain't got nothin'."

"Yeah," another Orbin said. "We ain't even got weapons to fight with."

"But guys," Vit said, "I was doin' it fer youse 'cause if we own the forest, then youse guys could get rich."

"Youse wasn't doin' it fer us. Youse was doin' it fer yer own self!" screamed the first Orbin. Within seconds, the whole Orbin tribe had circled Vit as they yelled and threatened him.

In a dark corner of the cave, the Magician's form materialized. He watched the angry Orbins with great amusement and waited for the right moment.

Just as the furious crowd was about to lunge at Vit, the Magician screeched his evil laugh and stepped forward. With arrogant superiority, he strolled into their midst. All eyes were glued to this threatening creature as he held up his hands and signaled for quiet.

"Who're youse?" one of the Orbins asked.

"I'm the one who will make your dreams come true," he said, strutting around the cave.

"Yeah, yeah. We's heard all dat b'fore," another Orbin said, glaring with disgust at Vit.

"Oh, really? Have you seen this before?" the Magician asked as he shot his hand out in a flourish like a conductor. The cave transformed into an Orbin paradise before the Orbins could blink. The dark walls took on light as streaks of gold, giant rubies, emeralds, diamonds, and other precious stones shone into the gloom. Scattered around the cave were inviting hammocks covered with brightly colored coverlets. The cave almost looked like a palace.

A large assortment of cushions appeared across the ground, suggesting a life of ease and pleasure. Spears, swords, and glistening knives materialized in one corner. In the center of the cave floor, a massive fire blazed, complete with a roasting carcass. As if offering power, a throne was displayed along the wall opposite the cave entrance. Bright red velvet radiated a welcome softness, and across its back, Vit's name was written in brilliant gold letters that matched the chair's arms and legs.

"How'd youse do dat?" Vit asked as his eyes fastened on the throne with his name on it.

"How I did it is not important. This and more can be all yours if you do exactly what I say."

Vit eyed the Magician. "Yeah? So, what does we gotta do?" Vit asked.

"Relax," the Magician said as he strolled over to Vit's throne and sat down. "I'm quite sure you will enjoy the task I have for you." He crossed his long legs. "You know about the group traveling to see Zarlock."

"But they was killed in da fire," Vit said.

The Evil Magician uncrossed his legs, stood, and pointed toward the cave's far wall. With a tremendous flash, a black ray shot out of his finger and thundered into the opposite wall. There was a massive explosion as boulders and rocks spewed into the cave. Vit and his followers ducked for protection as the chunks of flying rock narrowly missed them.

"If I can destroy the wall of this cave with my powers, imagine what I can do to you if you do not wish to follow me," he said. His menacing finger pointed out at them as he towered over the cringing Orbins. "I am going to take over this world and another world besides," he said. Then turning to the Orbins, he said, "You will be in charge of this world while I am off conquering the other dimension. Does anyone want to argue with me?"

"N-n-n-no, your honor, sir," Vit said.

"Good," he said and threw his head back in his evil laugh. "Now, here's what I want you to do. I want to stop that creature from the other dimension from returning to his home." His eyes glared with threatening anger as he sat on the throne. "If he goes back, he'll warn everyone of my coming." Once more, he crossed his legs and made himself comfortable. "You did an admirable job of almost eliminating them, but they escaped the fire. That human creature has a Madra Stone to protect him."

The Magician fell silent. No one made a sound. They stood quietly, waiting for him to finish what he had to say.

His own powers were equal to that creature's Madra Stone. But, if the travelers also got Zarlock's talisman, their strength would be doubled, and the Magician would not be able to stop them. He couldn't go to the Zarlock himself—all that love and sweetness—no, this he could not stand. That was why he had not entered the Tewin's village. Love, compassion, and kindness, these forces caused him too much pain. He rose from the throne and strutted around the cave. "We cannot get the Madra Stone away from the boy," he said, "but we can get the talisman away from Zarlock. My powers, together with the talisman, will give me more potency than ever."

With evident pleasure, the Magician stabbed at the air with a warped finger. "I will be invincible." Spinning around, he pointed his twisted finger at Vit. "You will bring Zarlock's talisman to me." He glared at Vit. "Any questions?"

"No problem," Vit said. "Youse wants us ta get Zarlock's talisman to ya. Dat's gonna be a real pleasure. Dey's only one hitch. We can't swim across da river what separates him from us."

“Fool,” the Magician said. “Do you think with all my power, I would not be able to do something as simple as get you across a river?”

“In dat case,” Vit said, “let’s get started.”

Chapter 27

The Stoflie

Wixer pulled his body erect and gave himself a mighty stretch. “We better get a move on before it’s too late and the Magician beats us there,” he said between yawns.

Breem jumped up beside Wixer. “Come on, guys, we have a battle to win.”

“Look at that!” Cam said pointing to the deep, fast-moving river they had yet to cross. “Does everyone know how to swim?”

“No,” said Dwinda.

“Hold it. How’re you gonna get over that?”

“Oh, that’s the fun part,” Breem said. Putting his fingers to his mouth, he let out a shrill whistle.

From out of the sky, sailed four of the large, purple, and green creatures Cam had seen earlier at the fire. At close range, he noticed that the Stoflie bodies were covered with scales, almost like a fish. Yet, their purple stomachs were smooth. Their heads looked like a dragon's with numerous points on top, and their enormous black eyes shone with caring and compassion.

"Now, this is totally awesome." Cam said. "I've definitely never seen anything like this back home."

Beaming with pleasure, Breem said, "The Stoflie are really friendly and love to help whenever they can."

Cam walked over to the Stoflie, thinking of how to greet them and get them talking. "Hey, you guys look really great. Your purple stomachs almost look like silk. Thanks for putting out the fire. That was amazing."

In a soft female voice, the Stoflie closest to him said, "That's okay, we love to help. My name is Vruunda. Hop on, and I'll take you across."

Thrilled, he said, "You mean it? I can ride across the river on your back?"

"I sure do," Vruunda said. "My friends will take the others."

Just then, Dwinda stepped forward. "Well, actually, we're on our way to see Zarlock on the other side of the river. We were hoping you could take us the rest of the way."

"That's even better." a male Stoflie beside Vruunda said. His voice sounded like an adolescent boy's squeaking in excitement. "We will fly you right there."

The group was soon soaring in the sky to Zarlock. Cam felt like he was on a carnival ride with Marvel flying close by his side. Looking down on the ground from his perch, he watched as the riverbank gave way to a small, wooded area. That was followed by a shallow valley with a narrow sparkling brook running down the middle.

Cam was grateful these majestic creatures were giving them a ride. This way, they would be at their destination much sooner. Still, he was disappointed when Vruunda began to angle down toward the gorge. He didn't want the ride to be over so soon. Gently, the Stoflie landed in the center of the valley by a shallow, rambling brook.

Climbing from the Stoflie's back, Cam said, "Awesome. That was fun. Too bad it's over so soon."

Turning her large head toward him, Vruunda asked, "Would you like to do it again sometime after you've finished your business here?"

"Would I? That would be great."

"We can't hear you call from here, so if you want us, just come to the water and whistle. I'd be thrilled to take you for a ride anytime." Vruunda took off into the sky.

He hurried to where the others of his group were gathered. Dwinda was giving instructions. "Zarlock lives in a cave at the end of this shallow valley, over there." She pointed. "Follow me."

Leading the way, Dwinda took the group along a path with a gentle uphill slope. Within minutes they were all running for the large cave perched by the stream. The closer they got, the faster their pace became, so anxious were they to complete their journey.

Chapter 28

Zarlock

When the excited band of travelers burst in on Zarlock, he was curled up in the corner of his cave, fast asleep. The clamor of their entrance awoke him with a start. It was clear to Cam that Zarlock was confused by the onslaught of visitors. He sat on the edge of his bed for a minute or two to wake up his senses. Cam was surprised to see a short, round creature covered with soft orange-brown fur. He had expected a more powerful figure. Zarlock gave himself and enormous stretch. His left arm reached up into the air, while at the same time giving his right side a good scratch. Then with a shiver of pleasure, he repeated the process for the other side.

When Zarlock stood, Cam thought he looked more like a gnome than someone with such a high position in Worpple. Zarlock's short legs had knobby knees ended with enormous feet. Cam thought his head was strange. It had two bulging bumps on the top and large round turquoise eyes with enormous pupils flanked his broad, flat nose.

If Cam thought that was strange, Zarlock did something Cam did not expect. As if a part of his waking procedure, Zarlock put his head back, and sang scales in the same way singers do when warming up for a performance at Carnegie Hall. La la la la la la la, he sang out to the roof of the cave, then his voice went an octave higher, and he repeated the process la la la la la la la.

"Ah, that's better," he said as he looked around to see what had awakened him. "Dwinda, is that you?" Zarlock asked as he squinted in her direction and stuck out his neck for a closer view. "How wonderful to see you," his baritone voice was loud and clear when he finally got it going. "Why, I haven't seen you for almost a year." He and Dwinda shared a big hug as a big smile wrinkled his face and made his sparkling eyes all but disappear.

"Now that the journey's over, I'm very well, thank you," Dwinda said. "I've brought some friends with me to meet you. You remember Breem, always out for fun and adventure. We've certainly had lots of that on this trip."

Zarlock chuckled as he attempted to wrap his short arms around Breem's large body for a hug and ended up giving his back a pat instead. "Yes, of course, I remember Breem. You're the one who instigated the last visit here. I believe you wanted an adventure then too. From the shine in your eyes, I see you're still enjoying your world."

"Thanks, Zarlock. I sure am glad to be here. On this trip, I learned that there are times when it's best to curb my adventurous spirit, too."

"That's called maturity, Breem." The wise gnome laughed as he once again thumped Breem's back.

Dwinda turned to Cam to introduce him. "This is Cam, he's..."

"Well, well, a boy from the Earth world," the sage said. "Welcome, Cam. I'll bet you're having quite an experience here in Worpple." His arm reached up and rested on the Earth boy's shoulders.

Even though Dwinda had told Cam to relax, an awkward shyness overcame him, and his brain turned to mush. How was he supposed to act again? He couldn't remember. The annoying red crept up from his neck, and soon, his face matched his hair. Not now, he pleaded with his embarrassment, not now. This thought created new awkwardness, and his red glow deepened. Looking down at the ground, he said, "Thank you, Your Hon. ah, your Zarlock, sir."

The wise gnome's hearty laughter filled the cave as he gave the boy a gentle shove. "Ah, go on, I'm just me, so call me Zarlock like everyone else. I'm delighted to have you here."

Just inside the cave, Marvel gave a short "Whoop."

"Oh, my goodness," Dwinda said, "I almost forgot an important travel companion." Taking Zarlock's hand, she led him to the whooper. "This is Marvel. She's Cam's friend and has been an extremely valuable assistant. If it weren't for her, we would probably not have completed our journey."

"A whooper!" Zarlock said, and his eyes became huge round balls. "How wonderful. It's a special treat to have you here. Welcome, Marvel."

Marvel came out with a soft purring sound as she flew over by Cam.

At last, Dwinda turned to the final member of the group. "And this is Wixer. He has a lot to talk to you about."

Wixer's head hung down, and his shoulders sagged as he said, "You may not want to welcome me after you find out what I did. I've caused a lot of problems and put everyone's life at risk."

Although Zarlock would have needed a ladder to give Wixer a welcoming hug. He was able to reach his arm up and pat his back. "Wixer, there's nothing you could do to cause me not to welcome you. That's why I'm here—my job is to help others in whatever way I can."

The old master led everyone out of the cave to a soft grassy area in the sun. He settled on the ground in a place that looked like it was well worn. The grass was soft sand, and the place where Zarlock sat had a small rise to support his back. "Please make yourself comfortable and tell me all about what brought you here," he said to his company as he stretched out his legs, crossed his ankles, and laced his hands behind his head.

"I guess I'll start," Dwinda said as she sat by a large boulder. The group settled in a circle as Breem plunked his ample body between Cam and Dwinda, and Wixer parked himself on the other side of Cam. All sat listening as Dwinda began their story and Julie's warning of evil coming to their land. Cam and Breem spoke up to explain the parts that involved them. Finally, Wixer took over from where the others left off.

"When these guys came to my cabin and told me what I'd done, I was shocked. I'm so sorry that I did that spell," he said. "Now I've caused all this trouble. I'm extremely worried the Magician will make good on his threats to kill Cam. I'm determined to do all I can to make things right again. At least, I've learned a valuable lesson—not to let my temper get the best of me."

Chapter 29

The Plan

Zarlock's wrinkled brow became creased with even more layers of wrinkles as he listened to their story. When they finished, he got up, clasped his hands behind his back, and circled the group. His large bushy tail swished in the air and his head stared down at the ground in deep thought. "It sounds as though you had quite a perilous voyage coming here," he said as he stopped and reversed his direction. "It's a good thing all of you arrived safely, thanks to Marvel," he said as he looked at the beautiful butterfly.

"I'm thrilled you came to me with this problem." He stopped and raised a finger straight up in the air, "You know, I've been getting a sense that all was not right with our beautiful world. This bad feeling was getting much stronger right here." He poked his finger at his stomach. "I suppose I was picking up impressions of the Magician as he got closer."

"Can it be fixed?" Wixer asked. "I couldn't stand it if nothing could be done."

Zarlock's wrinkled brow crumpled upward as the wise gnome smiled at Wixer. "You're being too hard on yourself," Zarlock said.

"It's true you did something that would have been best left undone. Yet, in some ways, good things have come out of this for you."

"Good?" Wixer asked.

"Sure. If you hadn't done that spell, you would never have met these wonderful new friends. You'd still be sitting at home feeling rejected and alone. Now, I'm not saying that what you did was right, but it might help you to look at it from another perspective." After a short pause, Zarlock said, "Your actions just reflected a lack of understanding, that's all."

"You're right," Wixer said, "I don't understand."

Zarlock once more sat in his place and explained to Wixer. "You were feeling alone in the world. In reality, no one's ever completely alone."

Wixer's eyes narrowed in confusion as he stared at the old wizard. Zarlock had everyone's complete attention as he continued. "The whole universe is united into a great rainbow of power. Even though we may sometimes feel alone, we're always connected."

"You sound just like Julie," Cam said. "She talked about Rainbow Energy. She said it's a life force that unites us and is shared with all living things."

"Exactly so. Cam, you've learned your lesson well." Turning to Wixer, Zarlock asked, "Where's that book now, Wixer?"

"It's here. I brought it with me. I'm hoping there's an answer in it on how to fix this mess."

"Nah," Zarlock said as he waved his hand at Wixer. "I am afraid no answers will be found in that book. Still, it's good you brought it with you. Now we can get rid of the book and the Magician once and for all."

"You sound as though you know about this book, Zarlock," Dwinda said.

"I've been told there was an event much like this many, many years ago."

Cam saw the wisdom shine in the gnome's eyes, and he understood why they had come here.

"It was before Zarlocks were appointed, and the same Magician came to Worpple to cause misery and pain. Indeed, it was during this experience that we discovered Rainbow Energy."

Zarlock stopped talking and looked wistfully out over the land as if he could actually remember that time.

He turned to his visitors, "We learned that although rainbows appear to have many different colors, in reality, it's just one, wrapped up in a prism of wonder and beauty. When we shine a light on a prism, it breaks up to give us a rainbow. But, in reality, it is all coming from the same place. Once we realized this, we named our connection to all of life Rainbow Energy, because we too are connected, just like the colors of the rainbow."

A refreshing breeze fluttered in the air and ruffled Zarlock's hair, giving him a mischievous appearance. "When the Magician tried to take over Worpple, the inhabitants of that time were not getting along. Arguments and fights were going on all over the land. With the Magician trying to cause pain and harm to everyone, the creatures of Worpple were forced to work together to find a way of ridding themselves of his wickedness. There had to be something that would help them conquer this evil force. Still, every idea that was tried had no effect."

Cam was surprised to watch a bright green cartoon bird come and sit by Marvel and quietly listen to Zarlock's story. Then as though the bird brought a small avalanche of curious creatures, Cam watched as little animals came out of the underbrush, sat around Zarlock, and listened to him talk. The wise old gnome patted some of the creatures as he continued his story.

"It began to look as though nothing could be done, but the situation was too serious to just give up, and everyone kept searching for a solution. As the different groups started working together, they found they actually enjoyed each other and could achieve more at the same time."

Chuckling to himself, he added, "Would you believe that even the Tewins and Orbins became friends? This cooperation grew and grew. For reasons, no one could understand, the Magician's evil power became weaker and weaker. It was really quite strange. The nicer everyone was with each other the weaker the Magician's powers became. It was at that point that Mootkee, the one who would eventually be the first Zarlock, realized that they had stumbled upon the greatest force in the world. To make sure that cooperation and friendship were making the difference, why not try an experiment? she thought. So, she came up with the idea of what has come to be known as the Rainbow Energy ritual."

"What's that?" Cam asked as he leaned back and propped on his elbows.

"The Rainbow Energy ritual is sort of illustrated in many of your activities on Earth. Your people, as well as ours each, enjoy playing games. Most games, whether they are card games, board games, or sporting games on an open field or a rink of ice, involve cooperation."

"Yeah, I love football," Cam said.

"Well, for your football to be successfully played, each individual player must give his or her best effort and support to the others on the team. If someone gives only half an effort or wants all of the attention for themselves, then the game will be lopsided, and that team won't win."

Just then, a fluffy leaf from a nearby umbrella tree danced in the air and landed on Cam's head. Cam sat quietly with an orange fuzz decoration on his head as he listened to Zarlock.

"Cooperation is only a part of the story. It's also vitally important to show our appreciation and love for one another. Things just go better in life when everyone is shown appreciation and works together. Also, when others know we appreciate them, it has a magic effect. It expands to the next person and the next until the whole world is affected. That's what we mean by Rainbow Energy Ritual."

Zarlock paused and plucked the fluffy leaf from Cam's head. Everyone watched as it turned to a brilliant purple. Then Zarlock reached over and put it behind Cam's ear.

"There, that's better," he said with satisfaction. "Now, Cam, do you understand what I've been saying?

"I sure do, and it sounds like a neat idea. I wish it was more like that at home."

Zarlock nodded. "Mootkee and her friends tried an experiment. Every night the creatures of Worpple gathered in groups for an hour. They concentrated on the positive energy and the One life-force. Some celebrated with music and singing, others danced, and some prayed and meditated. Gradually the Magician became so feeble that Mootkee was able to banish him to Petkula, a deserted place far from Worpple. That experience taught the inhabitants of Worpple that cooperation and caring for one another are powerful forces. We continue having Rainbow Energy rituals and understand more about the positive power within each one of us. Through doing these rituals, we now know the greatest force of all."

Cam looked around. Everyone was entranced by Zarlock's story, especially Dwinda. Then he remembered her telling him that she hoped to be a Zarlock someday. "I'm a little confused. What's the greatest force of all?" he asked Zarlock.

Even though his eyes were gentle, there was a power in Zarlock's voice. "Love, Cam. It's love."

He shook his head and said, "No way. How can mushy love get rid of the Magician and save the world?"

"Love is the biggest part of the Rainbow Energy," Dwinda said.

"The love I'm talking about must be pure and unselfish," Zarlock said. "It involves being consciously aware of our connection to all. It's the willingness to reach out and do something for others, even if we don't get anything ourselves."

Listening to the wise words, Cam recalled a flash of his last night in his home, and the sting of shame flared through him. He was aware of how unwilling he had been to do anything for his family.

Pausing to glance at the faces around him, Zarlock continued, "But, Rainbow Energy alone isn't enough to do the job. Oh my, no. We must be aware of how we are all connected by an invisible force combined with the conviction that the situation can be fixed. That's what's required to conquer the Magician...all the love you have within you. You'll be amazed at what miracles happen then. You'll be able to use that force to accomplish just about anything."

"Anything?" Wixer asked.

"Well, a great many things." Zarlock amended his statement. "Still, against the Magician, these three elements are an even more powerful weapon. Love, joy, and happy emotions that signal a strong measure of Rainbow Energy are things the Magician simply cannot stand. That's why he tried so hard to stop you before you got here. He knows I'm aware that with enough positive energy, the Magician would be totally powerless."

Cam remembered Julie telling him that he, Cam, had a force within him. He learned something about this force's power when he was freed from the tree limbs and vines. Now, Zarlock talked about the potency and hidden power of combining awareness of unity, cooperation, and love into Rainbow Energy.

"Now, my friends, there's no time to lose," Zarlock said, as his round body leaped from the ground. "We must ask for the help of all the creatures of Worpple. We must put the Rainbow Energy Ritual into action tonight." Turning his attention to Marvel, Zarlock spoke gently to her. "From what I've heard, it sounds as though you've been well-named. You are indeed a marvel. Yet again, we need your help."

Marvel offered a quiet agreeing Whoop and listened carefully to what Zarlock was saying.

"Go as quickly as you can to an area where Julie can read your thoughts. Even though you can't speak with us, I know Julie can understand you clearly. Tell her to ask every living soul in her part of the world for their help. At the exact moment the sun goes down tonight, they must all concentrate on the Rainbow Energy Ritual." Zarlock paused. He turned back to Marvel and continued. "It's essential that they allow themselves to be totally filled with the awareness of unity." Zarlock held up his finger to the sky. "Also, have her ask them to actually envision Worpple as the peaceful and joy-filled, loving world that it is. Everyone must concentrate as hard as they can. Do you understand the instructions?"

Marvel came out with a short Whoop and flipped over in the air, indicating her understanding.

"All right, go with speed and our blessings," Zarlock said.

The group stood in the bright sun and watched as Marvel took off on her mission.

"We must go to the river and ask the Stoflie for their help." Zarlock directed the others.

The group scurried up the side of the ravine and headed for the river.

Chapter 30

Theft

From a clump of bushes, Vit and four of his men stepped out into the clearing in front of Zarlock's cave. They had known Zarlock for a long time and didn't believe all that mumbo-jumbo about love power.

"What luck. Ain't nobody here." Vit said, rubbing his hands together in glee. "Dem stupid travelers should'a never told us where they was goin'."

Gathering his men around him, Vit said, "Listen ta me. Dem guys proba'ly gave Zarlock a line about needin' ta save da world. Dat's jist a way fer 'em ta rule with dat Rainbow stuff. Purdy soon we's gonna be da rulers o' this here world," Vit said and laughed. "'Cause the Magician said so, an' he's way more powerful than Zarlock.

"But, if he wants to use dat love power stuff, he's always talkin' 'bout, he's gotta have dat der talisman. Only when he comes to get it, it ain't gonna be der. 'Cause, we's gonna take it. Then I'm gonna be da powerful one."

"Scam and Sting, youse guys come with me ta search da cave,"

Vit said to the men closest to him. “Youse other two, stay out here an’ keep watch. Come on, let’s go.”

Stealthily, Vit and his men entered Zarlock’s cave. Vit pointed and whispered his directions to his men. “Scam, yer gonna look ta da left. Sting, yer gonna do da right. I’m gonna take da back.”

Vit slunk to the back of the cave and began throwing Zarlock’s personal items around. His search was an easy one. Zarlock had so few possessions it didn’t take Vit long to find the purple velvet box containing the talisman. It was on a shallow ledge just above his head.

Vit reached up, snatched the box, and peered inside. There he found a magnificent, ruby-red stone on the end of a sculptured crystal and gold wand. The stone glowed in the dimness of the cave and lit up Vit’s ugly green face in the gloom.

“Got it,” Vit said to his men who were still searching, “Come on; let’s get outta here.”

The band of Orbins wasted no time hurrying out of the cave and heading for their beautiful new home.

Chapter 31

Another Lesson

Cam and Wixer were the first to reach the river, followed closely by Dwinda and then Zarlock. Poor Breem, with his short little legs and large body, came huffing and puffing far behind the others. When Breem caught up, Zarlock gave the Stoflie instructions similar to those he'd given Marvel.

"Tell them they must actually see a world of love, joy, and peace in their minds. Perhaps they could envision all the positive feelings they have for their families and friends. Or they could just see our world as a place of happiness for all." Pausing, Zarlock scratched his head and continued. "Go to the areas of the world where Julie's powers cannot reach. Relay this message to all the creatures that live in the forests and shelters. Maybe leave the Orbins out for now. We will deal with them later. After you tell them what to do, ask them to spread the word to as many as they can reach. We have to get the message out quickly."

The Stoflies were thrilled to be asked to help in such a crucial undertaking. "We understand the seriousness of this mission," one Stoflie said for the group. "Thank you for asking us to help. We'll leave right away." The sky was filled with the magnificent sight of the Stoflie's beautiful iridescent wings shining in the sun and their purple and green bodies flashing with their movements. With great flourish, each of the Stoflie flew off in different directions as they searched out the areas where Julie could not reach.

After watching the majestic creatures fly away, Cam turned to Zarlock and asked. "They're sure strange creatures. How come they're always so thrilled about doing things for others?"

Zarlock reached his arm across the boy's back and was just able to stretch to Cam's shoulder. "That's a wonderful story, thanks for asking. A long time ago, when the Magician was here the first time, the Stoflies learned an important lesson. Whenever they had an opportunity to do something for another, they added joy into the Rainbow Energy we talked about earlier. Doing things for others made the Stoflie feel joyful while at the same time, the ones who were being helped were happier. It was contagious. There was more laughter, and everyone expressed their love and cooperated with each other even more. So, you see, for the Stoflie, helping another is also seen as helping themselves."

Zarlock turned and headed back to his cave, the troop of travelers by his side. "Another thing they noticed," Zarlock said, "whenever they did something nice for another, the kindness grew. With each generous act, the one receiving the kindness also tended to do a good deed for someone else. One time a Stoflie helped carry a Tewin to get medical help when he was sick. When that Tewin was better, he volunteered to design a bridge over a rushing river. Then others volunteered to build the bridge. Now all the creatures on both sides of the bridge have established a wonderful relationship. The kindness of the Stoflie became as contagious as a cold. Before long, Stoflies were known as the kindest and most helpful creatures around. Although, the Stoflie don't accept this identity because they say that while they may have been the first to discover the kindness principle, it applies to all the creatures everywhere."

Cam felt a little tingle deep in his heart as he realized he had just been given another vital lesson.

Without pausing, Zarlock turned and spoke to the group. "Breem, Dwinda, and Wixer, would you please collect the small blue herbs growing on the side of the ravine where I live? When you each have two handfuls, bring them to me. Cam and I will be at the circle above my cave."

To Cam, Zarlock said, "I'll need your help purifying the talisman. Come with me to the cave, and we'll begin."

Chapter 32

Missing Talisman

After the wizard and Cam reached the cave, Zarlock instructed, "Just wait here for a moment, and I'll get the talisman."

Cam waited idly, watching the wise old gnome from the doorway. Before Zarlock had gone three steps, Cam saw a worried expression spread across his face—it was clear that someone had been there. What had once been Zarlock's bed was now lumps of straw thrown around the room. His personal items were scattered everywhere.

Zarlock rushed to the back of the cave, stopped abruptly, and dropped his head low. He slowly turned and walked out of the cave with his shoulders slumped as he stared at the earth. As he walked, he looked over the mess left lying everywhere. Zarlock jerked to a stop for something on the ground and bent to pick it up before leaving the cave.

Once outside the cave, Zarlock flung his head back and bellowed. "Everyone, stop what you are doing and come immediately." His strong voice echoed down the ravine.

Everyone on the side of the ravine dropped the herbs they had collected and started running as they heard the urgency in the sage's voice.

"Something terrible has happened," he said once everyone was there. "My talisman has been stolen."

"Why...who would do such a thing?" Breem asked.

"Oh, I know who," Zarlock said as he held out his hand for the others to see. Lying in his palm was the tip of a purple claw.

"I wish those creeps would just delete themselves," Cam yelled angrily.

"That doesn't make sense," Dwinda said. Giant tears formed in her eyes and rolled down her cheeks. "Don't the Orbins realize they're in danger too?"

"Perhaps they don't believe the Magician is dangerous," Zarlock said sadly. "Anyway, even if they did, they tend to only think of themselves. Who knows? Maybe they think they can use my talisman against the Magician."

Throwing his stubby arms up in the air, he said, "Of course! I should have thought of it earlier. They were probably here on behalf of the Magician. I told you before the Magician can't enter into my space because good feelings cause him pain and make him shrivel up inside. Most likely, he has the Orbins working for him."

Dwinda said, "The Magician said he's going to Cam's dimension after he's finished here. Do you think the Orbins are in on that plan too?"

"That's a definite possibility," Zarlock said. "In that case, your world would be in even greater danger than ours, Cam."

Cam wasn't too worried about his world. He knew the powerful weapons they had. He was far more concerned about the innocent and warm creatures he had met in Worpple. "Doesn't your world have any guns or bombs or anything?"

"Our world has never had a war," Breem said to his friend from Earth. "Whenever we have a major issue, we either sit down and talk it out or come here to Zarlock for advice."

"Can't we do anything?" Cam asked. "We still have Rainbow Energy. Won't that be enough?"

"It's true, Rainbow Energy is the most important connection to the power," Zarlock said. "But it needs to be channeled in the right direction by using the proper tool, and that's my talisman. Before the sun sets tonight, we must devise a plan to get the talisman back."

"What about my Madra Stone?" Cam asked in the hopes of saving the situation. Then when he saw the look of surprise on Zarlock's face, he said, "Oops, sorry, I forgot about it. I guess I should have told you about it before. It had lots to do with our getting here safely too."

"You have a Madra Stone?" Zarlock asked, his face lighting up. "Wonderful. Where did you find it?"

"When I first arrived in this world and was walking with Breem to his school, I saw it on the ground." He dug it out of his pocket and held it out for all to see.

Everyone stared at the beautiful purple stone. Again, it glowed in Cam's hand as the colors swirled in their graceful dance.

"Can we use it instead of the talisman?"

"I don't know. Put it in my hand and see what happens," Zarlock said.

Gently, Cam placed the stone in the old man's hand and watched as the Madra Stone's colors simply disappeared. It had become nothing more than a smooth beach stone.

"Just as I expected." Zarlock handed the stone back to Cam. "I'm afraid the power in this stone is yours alone."

"So? I'll use it to get rid of the Magician." Cam stuck it back in his pocket.

"I'm not so sure about that," Zarlock said. "It takes special training to collect positive energy and direct it." He paused before continuing. "And, I don't know about your Madra Stone, but the incorrect use of my talisman could be hazardous." Rubbing his stubby hands across his worried brow, Zarlock said, "If my suspicions are right, the Magician not only has his own magic but the power of my talisman as well. The combined strength could be exceptionally tough to defeat. The Madra Stone alone may not be enough to overcome the strength he likely now possesses."

"There's one thing you should understand, Cam," Zarlock said as he squinted at Cam. "Evil lives within the negative thoughts and images a person has. This is the secret of the Magician's power. When people think about bad or unhappy things, they attract more sorrow to them like a magnet. The Magician knows this very well and uses those bad thoughts like a tool."

The group stood in a cluster listening to their leader. "When you're around the Magician's wickedness, you will have greater power if you keep your mind only on good or happy thoughts. The Magician uses the fear, anger, and sorrow of others as a power to bring about things like the dead animal coming to life or the fire that almost destroyed you at the Orbin camp."

Zarlock picked up a piece of blue herb, dropped by someone. As he rubbed the leaf with his thumb, he continued his lesson. "The only way to overcome the Magician's evil is to have great courage and face your fears head-on. Never forget that, Cam, focus your mind on joy and the delights of the world. Think about a happy puppy or the beauty of a rainbow, and your power over evil will be increased."

Cam stood with his mouth gaping open. "You mean the powerful weapons in my world wouldn't stop the Magician?"

"Oh, my, no!" Zarlock said dropping the blue herb. "They would give him even more power over you."

"How come?"

"The weapons in your world were developed through fear, hate, anger, and greed," Zarlock said. "Those are the exact emotions that give the Magician more power. If he were to come to your world, his strength would increase until he truly would be invincible."

"I was worried about the Tewins 'cause they didn't have any weapons and seemed so helpless. From what you're saying, they actually have a huge weapon against the Magician."

"That's right. The Magician would never dare to enter the Tewins' village. He would shrivel up and die with all the warmth and love those creatures have."

"Thanks, Zarlock. I'll never forget what you've told me. I guess the bottom line is we still need to get the talisman back."

"What do we do now?" Breem asked.

Wixer, who had been listening nearby, said firmly, "I'm going after it."

Everyone turned at the same time to gape at him.

Astonished, Dwinda asked, "But Wixer, how can you? It's too dangerous."

"I've been thinking," he said as he stood. "None of you can cross the river safely, but I can get across easily. My cape acts as a float in water. I'll find those little weasels and get the talisman back."

"What if it's the Magician who has the talisman and not the Orbins?" Zarlock asked. "You aren't powerful enough to deal with him alone, Wixer."

"I'm responsible for this whole mess. I said I would do whatever was necessary to make things right again, and I meant it."

Looking to the west, Wixer said, "I don't want to waste any more time talking. From the position of the sun right now, I have about an hour or so. If I hurry, I should be back by sunset."

"I'm coming with you," Cam said.

"But, little buddy," Wixer said, "what about the river and the Orbins? Not to mention the Magician, he wants to kill you."

"Yeah, right. Look who's talking, hero. I'm a good swimmer. I passed all my badges. Anyway, if I have trouble getting across, I'll just hang onto you. Don't forget, I have the Madra Stone, let's face it, you need me."

Zarlock stood, listening to the debate between them. He was impressed by their courage and sense of responsibility.

"It looks like Cam's determined," Dwinda said.

Breem laughed from his position beside his new friend. "I haven't known Cam long, but I've already learned that when he says he's going to do something, there's no stopping him. Right, Cam?" Breem gave him a little poke with his elbow.

"It looks like it's decided," Zarlock said with a hopeful look. "All the best, Wixer," he said as he shook hands with the gentle giant. "You've already redeemed yourself in my eyes. Good luck to both of you."

Seconds later, Cam and Wixer were racing toward the river. Behind them, they heard calls of "watch out for the Magician," "all the best," and "hurry back." It only took them a few minutes to get to the river, and without pausing, they leaped into the water. Fortune was on their side, and the current of the river landed them close to their destination. Without a pause, they scrambled onto the shore and broke into a run for the Orbins' camp.

Chapter 33

The Cardons

A Stoflie had just paid a visit to the Cardons with the directions from Zarlock. Everyone in the settlement became busy going about their preparations for the appointed time when they must focus their thoughts on Rainbow Energy. It was at this moment that Wixer and Cam burst in on them.

Two steps into the settlement, Wixer came to an abrupt stop. His mouth hung open in shock. There before him was a whole tribe of individuals that were identical to him.

"Hey, Wixer," Cam said excitement bubbling his words to the surface, "these guys look just like you."

"I never knew there were others like me anywhere. I thought I was the only one."

"Terrific!" Cam patted his friend on the back. "Now, you have a family."

Hearing Cam's cry, one of the gentle giants stopped chopping wood and came over. "How can I help you?"

Completely forgetting his original mission, Wixer asked, "Who are you? How long have you lived in this place?"

"What are you talking about?" the bewildered woodchopper asked.

Cam understood the confusion and jumped in, "It's okay. He's Wixer, and I'm Cam. Wixer's lived most of his life alone beside the Moving Forest. He didn't know there were others like him in the world."

"Really," the fellow said as he grabbed Wixer's hand and began pumping it in an enthusiastic welcome. "My name's Stang, and we're the Cardons. We've lived here for as far back as memory will take us."

Grinning broadly, Wixer said, "Oh my goodness, I forgot." "The Orbins have stolen Zarlock's talisman..."

Almost before Wixer could finish his statement, Stang grabbed his arm and directed them, "Quick, come with me."

Stang rushed to the center of the settlement, where a large gong hung. He picked up a mallet and struck the chime with a mighty force. Seconds later, the whole population of the Cardon settlement surrounded them. Standing among these giants, Cam felt small, although he knew he was among friends and was delighted to be a part of this crowd.

"A short time ago, a Stoflie was here to ask our help in a critical matter," Stang said to the group. Indicating the visitors, he continued, "Our new friends, Wixer and Cam, have told me the Orbins have stolen Zarlock's talisman."

A murmur of concern rippled through the crowd.

"Without it," he said, "the evil force that has infested our world cannot be eliminated."

"The Orbin's camp burned down," Cam said. "We don't know where they are."

"Don't worry," one of the giants said, "we know all of their hideouts." The Cardons chuckled.

"There isn't much time before the setting of the sun," Stang shouted. "All right, everyone, search the area. Bor, you take your group and search the marshes. A'Ella, you take Wixer and Cam in your group and go to the caves. I'll cover the north with my group. If anyone finds them, give your special call, and we'll come running. Come on, everyone; let's get that talisman back to Zarlock."

Not knowing where to go, the newcomers waited for further instructions. From behind, they heard a female voice, "Wixer and

Cam, come with me."

Cam watched as Wixer turned toward the voice. His friend was transformed. His huge eyes softened, and his enormous shoulders dropped as if the tension in them were melting away. It was clear to Cam that Wixer was attracted to A'Ella.

He glanced toward A'Ella. To him, she looked like any other Cardon. But then, how was he to know? He was a human boy. He couldn't tell what was beautiful in the eyes of a Cardon, and Wixer was fascinated. A'Ella's fur was a soft honey-blond, and around her neck, she wore a bright red scarf. Thick lashes fringed her enormous warm blue eyes.

It took Wixer a few seconds to find his voice. "If the situation were different, I would definitely like to get to know you better," he said to A'Ella. Then coming to his senses, he straightened and said in a business-like fashion, "Lead the way."

As A'Ella's group raced toward the north, they were confronted by low cliffs with a series of caves sprinkled along the face. "Zam and Gar—you go left," A'Ella whispered. "Tras and Wid, you take the right caves. Wixer, you and Cam come with me to the middle ones."

The threesome moved cautiously up the cliff and came to a ledge with three caves. A'Ella motioned for Cam to go to the left and Wixer to take the middle one as she headed to the right.

Chapter 34

Cave Hunting

Cam's cave was shallow, slightly more than a hollow in the rocks. He learned no one was there and decided to join Wixer. Once inside the middle cave, he had to wait until his eyes adjusted to the darkness surrounding him. Off to the right, he saw an entrance that appeared to lead deeper into the cave. From there, he heard Orbin sounds.

He pressed himself against the wall and crept into the side entrance. There, just five feet away, stood Wixer, as still as a statue, with his hands on his hips, staring into the cave. Cam advanced toward Wixer. As he neared, he too stopped dead in his tracks.

"I don't believe it," he whispered in astonishment. "I gotta be seeing things."

"Then we're both seeing the same things." Wixer's deep voice whispered back.

Orbins were sprinkled around the top of the cave, suspended from the ceiling by the top of their heads. It looked like they were stuck up there in a wild game with Krazy Glue. Some Orbins had their hands on the ceiling and were straining and kicking. Using all their strength, they were trying to loosen the invisible grip that held them. Others' arms and legs thrashed in the empty air, frustrated with their situation.

Cam and Wixer started to enter the cave with the Orbins when they heard a sound from behind. Grabbing his buddy, Wixer pressed them into a crevice in the cave wall and prepared to pounce, if necessary. Just as they were ready to jump, A'Ella came into view.

Creeping into the cave, A'Ella saw the Orbins before she saw Cam and Wixer. "Oh no, this cannot be."

"My sentiments exactly," Wixer said, stepping out of the shadows.

At the sound of Wixer's voice, A'Ella turned and screeched in surprise, then seeing that it was Cam and Wixer, she began to laugh, "Oh, it's just you two. You scared me."

Inside the cave, Vit heard A'Ella's cry and began to call out, "Help! I'm stuck. I can't get down."

A'Ella laughed and strolled into the cave. "What have you got yourself into now, Vit?"

"A'Ella, get us down. We's stuck." Then Vit saw Wixer and Cam entering the cave behind A'Ella, and a look of dread crossed his slimy features when he recognized them.

Cam and his friends were enjoying themselves immensely. No one rushed to reassure the Orbins—that would spoil the fun.

Leaning over to her companions, A'Ella whispered. "This is just too funny—I've got to call the other guys to come and see it."

As A'Ella headed out of the cave, Vit began screaming. "A'Ella, come back! Youse ain't gonna leave us like this." Panic rose in his voice.

Cam wasn't anxious to be left with the screeching Orbins and followed A'Ella part of the way out of the cave. After his last encounter with them, he didn't trust them for one moment and felt safer away from them until her return. She seemed to know how to handle them.

Once clear of the cave, A'Ella gave a few shrill cries that sounded like a cross between a dog's yelp and a screeching bird. Then she laid the red scarf from around her neck at the cave's entrance, put a stone on it to keep it there, and returned to the Orbins.

Back in the cave, A'Ella strolled around, assessing the strange sight. "Of all the situations I've seen you in, how did you manage this one, Vit?"

Vit squirmed to free himself as he answered. “It were that Magician guy—he done this. He’s from da devil.”

“What were you doing with Zarlock’s talisman?” Cam asked.

“We was jist borrowin’ it. We was gonna give it back—honest.” Turning to his men, he said, “Wasn’t we guys, dat were da plan, right?”

They half-heartedly mumbled, “Yeah, right boss, dat were da plan.”

“See. We’s jist wanted ta see how it worked. So youse is gonna get us down now, right?”

“Yeah, right,” Cam said. “Why am I having a hard time believing you? Where is it now, then?”

“I tolt ya,” Vit shouted. “That Magician guy took it offa us. Then he puts us up here an’ left.”

Wixer growled. “We don’t believe you. We think you stole it from Zarlock specifically to give to the Magician. We think the Magician asked you to steal it.”

“Now it’s starting to make sense,” A’Ella said as she wandered around the cave. “Doing a little home decorating Vit? New hammocks, some comfy cushions, a big meal cooking, and look at that throne. It even has Vit’s name in gold.” Getting angry, A’Ella asked Vit, “Is this what you were promised for getting the talisman away from Zarlock?”

Before Vit could respond, the cave filled with noise as Stang and the other Cardons joined them. As each of them entered the open area, they stopped and stared with open mouths at the scene before them, and the noise turned to howls and shrieks of laughter.

“Oh boy,” Stang said between belly-laughs as he reached up and tickled the Orbin’s dangling feet. “This is a good one. What happened?”

Once the roar calmed down, Cam said, “They say the Magician did it.”

“That’s right, and the Magician has the talisman,” Wixer said.

“Oh, no,” Stang said. “That’s not funny.” He turned to face Vit, and anger flashed in his eyes. “Vit, if you and your men ever hope to get down from there, you had better start telling us the whole story right now. Otherwise, we just might leave you up there to rot.”

“Honest,” Vit said, “we din’t do nothin’.”

“The Magician was in on it with them,” A’Ella said, spreading her arms to illustrate. "Look at this place. Vit even has his own throne."

"Okay, guys," Stang said angrily as he glanced at the luxury of the cave. "Let's get out of here. Leave them up there forever, for all I care."

Just as Stang swung around to leave the cave, several voices from above called out to him, "Don't go. We's gonna tell ya."

"All right," Stang said, as he eyed the suspended Orbins. "Who wants to go first?"

"It were him—him an' his big ideas," the first Orbin said, pointing a purple claw right at Vit.

"Stop! Stop!" Vit said.

"Yeah," another said. "Da Magician tolt him he was gonna be made into da ruler o' this here world if he done what he was s'pose ta."

Punctuated by cries of protest from Vit, the Orbins told the group standing below them their story.

"Right, we was s'pose ta get da talisman offa Zarlock an' give it to da Magician. But he," a third Orbin said, pointing at Vit, "he decided ta keep it fer hisself, so's he would be the powerful one."

"Then da Magician goes an' gets mad an' puts us up here," the first Orbin said, "And he takes off with da talisman."

"Ya stupid jerks," Vit said. "Now we's in even bigger trouble, 'cause da Magician is gonna be mad on accounta youse went an' tolt. Now he's gonna kill us."

"Don't worry, Vit," Stang said, "someone will get you down. But it will have to wait until Zarlock is free from his duties of ridding the world of the Magician." Then he said to his group, "Come on, gang, the sun will be setting soon. We have to go."

Everyone began to exit the cave. From behind, the group could hear the Orbins calling out. "Hey, youse guys, come back. Get us down. Don't leave us. The Magician's gonna come an' kill us."

Exiting the cave, Wixer turned to A'Ella, "What's going to happen with the Orbins?" he asked as he scooped up her scarf and handed it to her.

"I don't know, maybe we should leave them like that forever," A'Ella said with a twinkle in her eye as Cam, Wixer, and A'Ella all laughed. "Actually, as soon as this mess is over, we'll come back and try to help them down," she said.

When they reached the path leading down, A'Ella stopped to face Wixer. She took his hand and gazed deeply into his eyes. "I also look forward to getting to know you."

"All the more reason we must succeed/" He smiled and returned A'Ella's gaze.

A short distance away, Cam was getting impatient. Seeing them together reminded him of Marcy at home, and he felt a bit homesick. "Don't get too carried away, you two. You'll get plenty of time for that stuff later. Come on, they're leaving without us."

The Cardons were at the bottom of the cliff and hurrying away into the forest when Cam, Wixer, and A'Ella scurried down the cliff and rushed to catch up. They found the group standing in a circle just inside the forest.

Stang said, "We have to tell Zarlock what's happened. The sun's nearing the horizon, and we haven't much time. Anyone who wants to stay for the Rainbow Energy Ritual is welcome. The rest of you—come on, let's go."

Most of the Cardons raced for the river. A'Ella and Wixer ran side by side, while Cam worked at keeping up with Stang. As they were nearing the water, Cam heard his name being called from above. Vruunda, his Stoflie friend, soared in the air, landed on the water, and came close to where they were. Urgently, she called, "Quick Cam—climb on. I must get you to Zarlock immediately."

The group crowded around, and while Cam was climbing on, she said, "The Magician has taken Zarlock captive and is setting a trap for you, too. Zarlock asked me to get Cam there right away so he can use his Madra Stone. Unfortunately, the Magician knows I am coming for you, Cam, so watch for a special trap he has set. I'm sorry I can't take all of you."

Without hesitation, Vruunda swung up into the air as Stang called out to his friends. "There's no time to lose. We've got to get there immediately."

"Watch out for the trap," Vruunda shouted as she carried Cam up in the air.

Chapter 35

The Trap

From his perch on Vruunda, Cam looked around at the world spread out below him. He could see the Cardons swimming across the river. How graceful and smooth their movements were for such massive creatures. Toward the west, the sun was almost ready to set. The bottom of the enormous orb was just prepared to kiss the horizon.

Suddenly, he felt alone. He had been glad Wixer had come to Zarlock with them so that he could help fight the Magician, but if they didn't arrive on time, it would be up to him to save this wonderful world and the creatures he had come to love. A knot of fear formed in the pit of his stomach. What if he couldn't do it? What if the evil Magician took over the world? What if something terrible happened and it turned out to be all his fault?

Cam pushed the negative thoughts away. There was no time for him to dwell on his fears; he realized that Vruunda was dropping into the valley of the ravine. Cam reached into his pocket and pulled out the Madra Stone as his flying friend landed. He clutched the stone firmly, scrambled off the Stoflie, and dashed toward Zarlock's cave with a wave of thanks to Vruunda. As he neared the cave, for the third time this day, he was transfixed by the scene before him.

Zarlock was hanging from the limb of a large tree above his cave. A thick rope was tied around his body under his arms and looped over a thick branch. From the limb, the rope led away from Zarlock and stretched toward the ground. The other end of the line was in the grip of a gigantic monster. Its enormous bulging eyes and massive pointed teeth sent chills down Cam's spine. The hump on the monster's back forced its head forward and down between its shoulders. The hairy, burly body with the muscular arms was twisted and deformed.

Below, Zarlock was a diabolical terror waiting to attack. Directly under him was a large open pit filled with writhing, menacing-looking snakes. There were too many snakes for Cam to count as he watched their numerous heads thrust up from the opening toward Zarlock. There were red, green, and yellow reptiles—some had giant, flat heads, like a cobra from his world, while others were more like a rattler, with sharp-pointed mouths. Their slithery bodies hissed and writhed amongst each other like water in a boiling pot. Yet, above this terror, the old gnome's face wore an expression of peace and wisdom that shone in his large eyes.

Immediately behind the snake pit, on the right side of Zarlock's cave, Breem and Dwinda were tied to one another, back-to-back. Their eyes were filled with fear and shock. The Magician stood back from Zarlock's cave's left side, reveling in his satisfaction and power.

"Welcome, Cam," the Magician said, "I've been waiting for you."

Terror and anger engulfed Cam as he forced himself closer to the horrific scene. Suddenly, from out of the air, several ugly, black beasts blocked his way. They looked like seven-foot-tall rats that stood on their hind legs. They had short, stubby noses, amazingly long tails, thick leathery skin, and their beady red eyes glared at him. Rows of long, jagged, shark-like teeth that came to razor-sharp points filled their mouths.

More repulsive than the sight of them was their stench. Cam recoiled with an inner tremble. He gagged, trying to catch his breath as sweat-soaked his body. He was grateful he had not eaten for a while. His hands became almost too slippery to hang on to the Madra Stone.

"Oh, no!" Cam groaned, overwhelmed by fear. "How am I

supposed to do all this alone? I'll never make it."

As he clutched the magic stone, Cam wiped one sweaty palm down his pant leg and then switched hands to repeat the process with the other hand. Holding the Madra Stone out before him, he haltingly advanced toward the monsters. One beast's tail whipped out toward him and knocked the stone from his hand. As he scrambled to retrieve it, Cam could hear the Magician's evil laughter in the background.

"Did you think you could defeat me with that measly toy? With my own strength plus Zarlock's talisman, I have twice the power of that thing. Let it go, boy. You can never beat me now."

Cam found it easy to believe the Magician. Maybe the evil monster would win. Perhaps this was too much for him. Still, he clutched the Madra Stone close to his chest and scrambled to his feet. *I'm not going to go down without a good battle*.

Remembering his football moves, Cam rushed the brutes. He zigged and zagged his way through the wall they formed. Almost through the line…there…there's an opening to the right. Oh no, an ogre's tail wrapped around his ankle. He sprawled on his stomach and rolled onto his back. The Madra Stone was gripped to his chest like a football. That was when one of the beasts lunged at his throat.

Chapter 36

The Battle

As if by magic, the brute was flying away from him. Cam stared up at Wixer, who had arrived just in time.

As Cam scrambled to his feet, he looked around to see Cardons everywhere. They had the situation well in hand. Rat-like monsters were flying all around him. One monster lashed out with its tail to stop a Cardon's blows. The tail whipped itself around the Cardon's hand, but the giant grabbed a firm hold of the tail and whirled the beast in the air like a whip. As the monster spun, it crashed into two other monsters, and all three crumpled to the ground.

Cam rushed toward Zarlock and noticed the Magician's mouth moving as he shouted to the Cardons. The roar of the battle nearby prevented any sound from being heard. The Magician stabbed his finger toward the fight.

Looking back, Cam was afraid a new horror would harm his friends. He watched Wixer reach out to struggle with one of the black, leathery monsters when it vanished before him. Spinning around, he found all the beasts were gone.

However, Zarlock was still dangling over the snake pit. The

Cardons had been too occupied with the rat-like monsters to notice. Now the sight seemed to mesmerize them.

Taking a gulp of air, Cam once more held the Madra Stone out before him as he stood just a few feet away from the snake pit and Zarlock. Beyond the hole, Breem and Dwinda struggled with the rope wrapped around their bodies. Above Zarlock's cave, the sky showed the first bright streaks of brilliant color as the sun began to set.

Oh no! It's too late—the sun is setting, and everything is a mess.

"Remember what I told you about love and evil," Zarlock said. "Concentrate. Face your fears."

"Shut-up." The Magician screamed to Zarlock. Turning to Cam and the Cardons, he shouted, "If you come any closer, Zarlock is dead. One drop of venom from these snakes can easily kill the largest beast. Think of the agony they are going to give to your famous leader."

To the boy from Earth, the Magician said, "Thank you for bringing your Madra Stone to me. Now, hand it over."

"No." Cam backed away from the Magician.

"You will." The Magician sneered.

The Magician pointed his gnarled finger toward the enormous monster holding the rope connected to Zarlock. He gave a slight movement of his finger.

Zarlock yelped as he began to slip down toward the snakes. The Magician teased Cam by again twitching his finger. This time Zarlock's weight jerked to a halt, just barely out of reach of the slithering mass below him. The snakes writhed and hissed in anticipation of their next meal.

"You have one last chance. Now, you stupid imbecile—hand over your stone or he dies."

What a bind. If he refused to hand the Madra Stone over, Zarlock would die. But if he gave it to the Magician, he knew he would be killed along with Zarlock. Either way, there did not seem any way out of this mess.

Above, he saw the colors of the setting sun growing brighter. The sky blazed with swirling shades of gold, purple, and brilliant fuchsia. The hour had come. All the creatures of this world were thinking of Rainbow Energy. If Worpple was going to be saved, it would have to be now.

A hush fell across the world, and Cam felt as though time stood still as the earth opened its arms to the glory of the love-power coming from the creatures of Worpple. Then, as if transported back in time, he recalled Zarlock's lesson about evil.

"There's one thing you should understand," Zarlock had stressed. "Evil lives within the negative thoughts and images of a person's mind. This is the secret of the Magician's power. When people dwell on the bad or the world's unhappiness, they attract more sorrow to them. The Magician knows this very well and uses those bad thoughts like a tool."

"Hurry up, boy. Give that stone to me now."

The Magician's words jerked him out of his thoughts. His stomach knotted as bile shot up his throat. "Tell me what to do," he yelled to Zarlock.

"Hold the stone up and remember the Rainbow Energy," Zarlock said.

From above the tree where Zarlock was tied, he heard a long, loud whoop.

At the sight of Marvel, Cam felt love surge through him for his fantastic friend. He realized that he had let his fear stop him from experiencing his Rainbow Energy.

Just then, things began to come together in his mind. When the Magician pushed him over the cliff, he had been fearful of his family's anger at his being gone so long. When he felt fury toward the Orbins, the Magician had started a fire. When everyone had shown fear of the Magician, he had taken over Zarlock's camp. And just now, when he had been angry and frightened, a group of rat-like monsters had sprung up in his way.

With these realizations, he felt a small shudder run through him like an electrical shock. He understood. His negative emotions were giving the Magician power. *Of course, the Magician lives off our fear, anger, and hatred.* In a flash, Cam understood all that Julie and Zarlock had told him about Rainbow Energy.

If this theory was correct, then he must concentrate on keeping his power right where it belonged, here inside of him. He thought about the life-force within him, his own share of Rainbow Energy. In that instant, he felt a part of him growing and spreading, like a giant rainbow cloud fanning out in all directions across the world.

Joy danced through his heart, and wonder filled him as love

poured out from him, going everywhere at once. Again, he understood that what Julie said was true. He was connected to all of life and maybe even the whole universe.

He was almost overcome with love for Marvel, for this beautiful land and its unusual creatures. He felt a sense of joy mixed with gratitude as he remembered his family back home. His heart swelled bigger as Marcy and his friends came to his mind. At that moment, he couldn't imagine wanting to live anywhere else in his world. He felt confident and strong as he lifted the stone up to the sky to transmit these marvelous feelings to the whole universe.

"Everyone, join in. Concentrate on the Rainbow Energy.'" Zarlock called to the watching Cardons.

Wixer reached down and took A'Ella's hand; then, along with the other Cardons, obeyed Zarlock's directive.

"Stop!" the Magician said as he lunged toward Cam. Before he had gone two steps, the Magician crumpled to the ground, groaning and writhing in pain. Such concentrated love and joy were just too much for him to withstand.

As Cam held up the Madra Stone, its deep purple began to glow even brighter. Sparks from the stone's swirling colors shot up to the sky.

"Nooo." The Magician screamed. He clutched at Zarlock's talisman, which had fallen to the ground. "Dark forces of diabolic night come to me now."

Without warning, the sky darkened. A strong wind filled the air. Slowly at first, then building and building, the wind grew until it became a gale. Dust swirled in the air and stung with tiny particles pelting Cam's face. Branches of trees and bushes whipped about as though in an angry fight.

Zarlock, tied to the tree, began bouncing even closer to the snake pit below him. With every rebound, the snakes reached up to grab hold of the close feet. Lightning flashed, and the whole world was soon engulfed in a great storm that threatened total destruction.

Cam watched as a flash of lightning struck close to Marvel. Now his mind was filled with his concern for his special friend.

"Concentrate," Zarlock shouted to Cam and the Cardons as he put his head down in focused thought.

With Zarlock's reminder, Cam was jarred back to the task at hand. Once more, he realized that this was just another of the

Magician's attempts to distract him from his mission. Again, he called to mind everyone and everything he cared about.

Was it from out of nowhere, or was it from everywhere? He could not tell. Specks of light caught his eye, like sparkling dots of diamonds in the air. The particles grew and grew until the atmosphere was filled with glowing, flashing prisms of brightly colored lights. Without being told, Cam knew the illuminations were from the positive energy being generated by the creatures of this world, and he was filled with awe.

That's when he realized why they had named this Rainbow Energy. The air was filled with flashes of beautifully sparkling colors. He was filled with wonder that this was coming from all the fantastic creatures he had met in Worpple.

At that moment, he knew that throughout the land, creatures big and small in every corner and crevice of Worpple were busy with their Rainbow Energy ritual. They were concentrating on the positive power and sending it out to the universe.

The lashing of the wind stopped, as if on command. The specks of colored lights began to come together to form one concrete, colorful, and radiant column. The colors started to shape themselves into a wondrous tower of pure energy. The brilliant luster of the impressive spectacle erased all signs of the storm that had threatened only moments ago.

Cam watched the incredible pillar begin to revolve in the air. Faster and faster, it turned until it resembled a whirling tornado of sparkling, glowing light. As though it were filling a vacuum, the column streaked toward the Madra Stone. The energy was swallowed by the stone, making it even more potent.

A tremendous scream filled the air. Cam's attention was ripped away from the stone and toward the origin of the shriek. There, a couple of feet away, the Magician again writhed on the ground in pain. Now the combined power of the Madra Stone and the loving Rainbow Energy was destroying the Magician.

Staring in amazement at the Madra Stone in his hand, Cam watched as the light energy that was entering it seemed to surge right out like a river and stream directly toward the Magician. As the rainbow of light surrounded the Magician, he screamed out his rejection of what was happening. A thought came to Cam, and he raced over to where the Magician thrashed on the ground in agony.

Compassion and yearning to help the Magician flowed through him. He wished this sad creature could feel the joy and wonder he felt. At that moment, he reached out to the Madra Stone with the intent of sharing what he sensed with the Magician. *If I give the Magician all the love of this land, I'll be able to help him.*

As if a lump of burning hot coal had touched him, the Magician's shriek pierced the air. Cam sprang back from the intensity of the howl. He watched in disgust as the Magician's body began to decay. In slow motion, the Magician disintegrated on the ground before him.

Nearby, he heard another cry. He jumped back to prepare himself for yet another confrontation. Instead, he saw Zarlock tumble to the smooth grassy ground below him. The pit of snakes had vanished along with the monster that held the rope.

Breem and Dwinda, too, were released from their bonds. Jumping up and down in joy, they grabbed each other and started bouncing round and round in excitement.

Before long, the whole area was filled with joy and laughter.

Lifting Cam in the air over his head, Wixer shouted, "You did it. You saved our world and destroyed the Magician."

Chapter 37

Victory Party

Perhaps it was the shock of all that had occurred, but it took Cam a few minutes to realize the battle was over, and he had won. Being carried around on the crowds' shoulders like a football hero helped bring the reality home. Before long, he too celebrated in joy along with those present.

"Put me down. Put me down." He laughed.

"Okay, little buddy." Wixer eased him to the ground. A'Ella reached over and gave Wixer a kiss on the cheek.

Cam went to where Zarlock, Dwinda, and Breem were rejoicing. The whole area was soon a jumble of action as everyone was jumping up and down in excitement and giving each other hugs and pats on the back.

Moments later, creatures from all over Worpple began to arrive. The air and ground filled with creatures all coming to bask in the victory. As if a great deal of planning had gone into the preparations, everyone was enjoying a giant celebration.

Some Cardons, who had stayed for the Rainbow Energy Ritual also arrived. "We were in the middle of doing the ritual," one Cardon said, “when we heard loud screams from the cave. We raced inside, thinking that something horrible had happened. And there were Orbins scattered over the floor of the cave. None of them had suffered any serious injury, except maybe to their pride. The beautiful cave decorations, including Vit’s throne and the roasting carcass, were gone.”

“Gee, that’s too bad,” Cam said and chuckled.

“You’re right,” Stang laughed. “Still, I’m pretty sure the Orbins will create new mischief another day.”

The Stoflie kept arriving with new passengers as the world's various creatures came to join the festivities. Food of more varieties than Cam even knew existed piled up outside Zarlock’s cave. After everyone had calmed down enough to eat, they sat down to the enormous feast.

When the eating was done and the ground had been cleaned, Dwinda called, “Hey Cam, I remember a promise of a bonfire we were going to have. This looks like a perfect opportunity.”

“Great idea Dwinda, thanks. Okay, everyone,” he took over the organization, “we need lots of firewood.”

Soon all forms of creatures were scurrying around bushes and behind rocks, searching for firewood. Groups of little life-forms teamed up in twos and threes as they coordinated their efforts to drag, lift or roll large pieces of wood to the designated fire site.

Wixer’s eyes shone with excitement and joy. A whole new world had opened to him, and he was about to make sure it would stay that way as he joined his new family. Turning to Zarlock, he asked, “Do you think this is a perfect opportunity to burn a certain spell book before anyone else can use it?”

“Great idea, Wixer,” Zarlock said. “Come on, let’s go get it.” Zarlock put his arm up Wixer’s back in the same casual manner he would use if he were tall enough to reach his shoulders, and they strolled together toward Zarlock’s cave.

Later that night, the group of travelers sat around a now-dying bonfire. Most of the little creatures had wandered back home to their comfy beds. Others were sleeping balls of fur curled up where they had been sitting. Most of the Cardons had gone home. And then there were those who were content to sit quietly and enjoy the starry night.

That was terrific, Cam." Breem smiled in satisfaction. "I don't think I've heard so many strange songs in my life. Where'd you get them all?"

"From summer camp," he said through a wide yawn. "I go every year. Someone's always bringing new songs."

Unable to stifle another yawn, he announced to the group, "I'm wiped. I'm going to bed. See you later."

"That sure was a great adventure," Breem sais to Cam's back as he walked away.

"Wonderful, Breem, thanks." He stumbled sleepily into the cave, followed by Marvel. Cuddled up to his special friend, he whispered, "Marvel, you are the best friend a guy could ever have. When it's time for me to leave here, I want to take you with me. Otherwise, I'll never see you again. Promise me that you'll come back with me."

In the darkness of the cave, all he could hear was a gentle Whoop, which sounded almost like a purr.

Chapter 38

The Next Day

Cam awoke slowly. "I wonder what's gonna happen on the return trip?"

In a flash, his eyes flew open like he had been stung by a bee. He sat up and stared around him. He was in his own bed at home. How could that be? Was it all a dream? What had happened?

Confusion, disappointment, and sorrow did an emotional swing through him. Dejected, he slumped on the edge of his bed. His excellent adventure had just been a dream. *But it felt so real*. After a couple of minutes, he grabbed his jeans and struggled into them. It was then that he noticed heaviness on one side. Reaching into his pocket, he was astonished to find the Madra Stone and the silky leaf-seeds right where he remembered leaving them.

Cam jumped up and held the Stone out in his hand. To his great pleasure, it was still glowing a rich, deep purple. The various colors within it swirled and twisted in their magnificent patterns.

"Wow! It's still working."

From the hall, he heard his mother's call and gentle knock on his door. "Cam, are you up?"

In a rush, he shoved the leaf-seeds and stone back into his pocket. "Come in, Mom."

His mother stuck her head in the door. "Your father's going to be here in a few hours. You'd better hurry to get that marsh water."

He stared at his mother—stunned. It was the same day he'd left to go to Worpple. No time had been lost at all. Again, he wondered if it had all been a dream. But no, he still had the Madra Stone, so he must have been in Worpple. Nothing made sense.

Stepping into his room, his mother asked, "Are you all right? You don't look good. Are you ill?"

"No, Mom, I'm cool." He smiled as he gathered himself together. "I was just thinking about my dream last night. I'll hurry."

Just then, Tara walked into his room without knocking. Cam finished pulling on his jeans as he said, "Hey, squirt, what's up?"

"You better hurry if you want to go with dad," Tara taunted.

"That's enough from you, young lady," her mother said from behind her. "You apologize to your brother right now."

"It's okay, Mom," Cam said. "She's just getting back at me about all the times I bugged her."

"What's with him?" his sister asked.

Later at the breakfast table, his little sister was shocked when Cam offered to make toast for her. "What got into you?" she asked. "Last night, you couldn't stand me."

Just then, a flood of memories filled Cam's mind. He realized that her bratty behavior toward him was her defense. He saw himself pulling her hair and pushing her when no one was looking. He realized that he had been a bully toward her, and she was just trying to defend herself. Now, things are going to change.

"Oh, I just thought it was time that things should change around here." He smiled as he put the bread into the toaster.

The next day, after he came home from a great visit with his dad, Cam was once again out in the field practicing his football moves. He reached down, scooped his ball from the ground, and noticed Marcy running toward him. As she ran, she waved a piece of paper over her head and yelled something he couldn't quite hear. By the time she reached him, she was out of breath, and her words were in gasps and puffs. "I was just at your house…your mom…asked me to bring this…to you right away."

Still clutching his football, Cam took the paper, tore off the tape at the top, and peered at the message. Without warning, he threw up his hands, sending the football and note flying in the air. He grabbed Marcy around the waist, lifted her in the air, and shouted, "Fantastic, I made it!"

She whooped her infamous laugh and cheered along with him.

He placed her on the ground and danced a crazy boogie all over the field. He barely stopped for breath between words as he said, "I did it, Marcy. I'm on the football team next year. The note says the coach just phoned and wants to see me for roll call on Monday after school."

"That's wonderful," she said. "You're on your way. You're gonna be a great football player."

"I'm so happy I can barely stand it. Hey, I could even like Jason right now."

Marcy came out with her strange whooping laugh. With the sound, he felt a mixture of joyful sadness rush through him. Her laughter reminded him so much of Marvel. Just then, a thought tickled the back of his mind. Was it possible? Could there really be a connection between Marcy and Marvel? Staring for a second at his friend, he dismissed the thought. It was just too silly to even consider. Still, he felt like he had experienced stranger things in the last little while.

As he watched Marcy, he noticed the huge smile on her face fade, and a look of anger and disgust replace the happiness that had been there. Looking around, he saw Jason coming across the field with his gang.

But his joy refused to fade. He believed that the events in Worpple were not just a dream. Otherwise, how could he have brought back the Madra Stone? Probably Zarlock had used his magic to create the illusion of a vision. Then, Zarlock had turned back the clock and left him with the stone. He could never know for sure. But this was how he made sense of the confusing muddle.

Confident that Worpple was not a dream, he knew he had just battled far worse than Jason's gang—and won. Now, if it were necessary, with the help of the Madra Stone, he could win again.

Cheerfully, he greeted Jason. "Hey Jason, what's up?"

"Who wants to know?" Jason asked, his words tinged with suspicion. He reached down and picked Cam's note up from the ground.

Cam considered taking it away from Jason and then decided that it was fine for Jason to read the message. Instead, he watched as Jason's face took on a look of utter astonishment. Turning to his gang, Jason said, "Blubber guts here made the football team for next year."

"How come he got in, and we didn't?" one of the boys asked as he threw his hands up in the air.

"You guys are off the team?"

"Yeah, that's right, fatso," Jason said. "Not that it's any business of yours."

Stepping closer to Jason, he said, "Too bad, I was looking forward to teaching you a few tricks."

Jason squinted at Cam. "I got a few tricks of my own that I can teach you." He gave Cam's shoulder a shove. "Hit me back. I dare you."

Without warning, Cam was sure he could hear Zarlock's voice in his head. "Remember what I told you about good and evil. Don't give away your power."

Cam remembered that the positive force, the Rainbow Energy, was the only way to work the Madra Stone. In fact, he realized that it was the only way to achieve any of his goals. Instead of striking out at Jason, Cam put his hand in his pocket and held the stone. Smiling, he remembered the life force he shared with all others, even Jason.

Seeing Cam's reaction, Jason reached out and shoved Cam, this time using more force. Just as he started to push, he lost his footing and tumbled to the ground.

Cam reached down and grabbed Jason's arm. "Let me help you up."

Jason got to his feet, yanked his arm free of Cam's grip, and lashed out with greater force. This time, the fist that was aimed at Cam's jaw not only missed, but Jason spun around and lost his balance. Once more, he ended up sprawled on the ground, face down.

For a second time, Cam put his hand out to help Jason to his feet. Before Cam's hand could reach him, Jason scurried across the ground on his hands and knees as if a monster were chasing him.

“Keep away from me,” the boy yelled. Fear filled his eyes as he scampered to his feet and rushed off the field. “Come on, guys,” he said to his friends, “Let’s get outta here. That guy’s weird.”

“No way, man,” one of his friends shouted. “He didn’t even touch you. What’re you runnin’ for?”

The rest of the group stared after him. Some of them had a look of disgust on their faces, while others shook their heads in disapproval. Slowly, each of them headed off the field, away from the direction Jason had gone.

Cam gave a secret smile. He knew exactly what was bothering Jason. Happily, he trotted over to where his football lay and picked it up. Then he walked over to Marcy and took her hand as they walked off the field together.

CPSIA information can be obtained
at www.ICGtesting.com
Printed in the USA
LVHW010916180821
695555LV00012B/1178